*Following Zippy*

Also By C.B. Burdette:

~Death by Numbers~

# Following Zippy

## C.B. Burdette

Flower Child Publishing

Published 2014 by Flower Child Publishing

ISBN 13: 978-0692245804
10:     0692245804

10  9  8  7  6  5  4  3  2

To Rosiebug. May you learn to always live your life to the fullest.

"Someone should tell us, right at the start of our lives, that we are dying. Then we might live life to the limit, every minute of every day. Do it, I say! Whatever you want to do, do it now! There are only so many tomorrows."

-Pope Paul IV

*Following Zippy*

# Chapter 1

Chalk screeched down the face of a green chalkboard as I sat in the back of the classroom.

I searched the room for a clock, and found it hanging over the threshold of the door. It was only a minute past seven. Walking in the door was Jake Jenkins. He had orange hair and pasty skin, and had obviously lost a battle with a good case of acne. He styled his hair like a porcupine with gobs of hair gel.

I would've assumed that Jake the jerk would've had the mole removed from his left cheek over the summer. Even more so, I would've assumed that Darla would've dropped him by the curb after realizing how much of tool he was. Then again, she had dated him since the sixth grade, so why would she decide to wise up now? I guess that's what drew me to her in the first place. As naïve as it was, she was always seeing the best in a person.

My hatred for Jake began in middle school. I was in the sixth grade and he was in the seventh. Girls had started using the term 'dating' along with the term 'boyfriend', even though no one actually went anywhere. Darla was as cute as the day I met her in third grade. She had shiny brown hair that traced the edges of her collar bone, and green eyes that made you feel like you were staring into a field of clover.

When we switched over from elementary school to middle school, the girls started becoming more distant from the boys. At least they did from the boys who were in the sixth grade. They liked the 'older' boys. Of course to an eleven year old a lot of boys are older.

Darla had stopped talking to me as much as she did when we were in elementary school. We didn't have any classes together but she'd still wave at me in between classes. Eventually I was so mad at her that I'd look away when she'd wave.

Halfway through the sixth grade school year I was walking through the hall and saw her talking at her locker to a seventh grader. Why a seventh grader even found his way to the sixth grade hall was questionable enough on its own but the fact that he was standing with Darla, the girl I loved, was even more questionable.

I hadn't talked to her in a few weeks. By this time I'd already been giving her the cold shoulder, but if some other boy was going to invade on my territory, it was probably time to start talking to her again. She was, after all, my best friend.

"Hey Darla," I said as I walked up to her and the guy.

The seventh grade ogre with a football hoodie looked at me, eyes reeking of 'eat crap and die'. "Who are you?"

"Jake, this is Gabe. We were friends in elementary school." Darla stared at me a little, "We don't have classes together so we haven't gotten a chance to really catch up lately. How's your mom?"

"Yeah, Gabe, how's your mom?"

"Gabe, Jake's on the football team. Maybe he could teach you some stuff and help get you on."

"Sorry, Darla, even if we did let sixth graders on the football team, we wouldn't let some skinny little urchin in."

"Urchin?" I said, "At least call me a shrimp."

"We're learning about the underwater food chain in science, and as far as I'm concerned, you're not even a shrimp. You're an urchin."

I stared at him wide-eyed before turning my focus back to Darla, "I'm sorry I've been ignoring you the past couple months in the hall. I just hated that we didn't have any classes together is all."

"It's fine," said Darla, "I thought you were mad at me. But hey, I gotta go to class, so tell your mom I said hey, ok?"

She walked off with Jake and he turned around, "Yeah, tell your mom I said hey."

Thus the moment I knew I would forever be appalled by the ogre named Jake. Darla and I stayed friends at a distant though, waves in the hall, but we never hung out again. When we got into high school we had a few classes together here and there, but never had quite the same friendship that we had when we were kids.

"Hey Gabe!" Darla said as she dropped her books on her desk. "I didn't think I'd luck out seeing you in the very first class on the veeeerrry first day back to school."

That's when she winked at me. Oh man. The Darla wink. The wink that sends every guy at Elmont High melting into a puddle of goo. The fact that Jake was sitting in the front row deterred me from winking, at first.

'What can a wink hurt?' I thought to myself.

I winked at her. I gave her my wink that's not really even a wink but more of a reason to believe that I could possibly have some horrible case of Tourette's.

"Gabe," Darla leaned in whispering, as her cocoa butter scent wafted through the air in my direction, "Gabe, I think you have something in your eye. I have a mirror if you want to use it."

Just then Jake came up and leaned over Darla and said loud enough so that he could make me look like a wimp, "Yeah Gabe, you might want to check your dainty little eye in my girlfriend's mirror. Must have some kind of girly mascara clumped up in it. Hah!"

Darla can turn me in a puddle of goo with a simple wink, whereas her evil boyfriend just turns me into a puddle of sewage waste just by shooting a look in my direction.

After class I caught Jake staring me down. I thought it would be a smart idea to bypass him by sliding out of the room and going to hide behind the door of my locker. Big mistake. Right when I thought I was hidden from the mass of what is known as Jake I peeked over the edge of my locker only to find his royal highness standing over me as domineering as a lion to a tiny mouse.

"Hi Jake," I squeaked. I squeaked like a mouse. I had a tendency of making myself look like a total weenie in front of him.

"I have no clue why Darla pities you so much. I also have no clue why you're so stupid to not know that you should leave Darla alone since she has a big beefy boyfriend who could squash you into a million little pieces just by poking you with his pinky finger. You know, I tried to be nice for the first few years, but now I've got Darla where she'll never leave me. I've put up with your googly eyes staring at her long enough and I think you should put them back in your head."

I attempted to pull my hoodie over my scraggly dark hair and walk away but just as I was closing my locker the string attached to the hoodie got slammed in my locker.

"So much for an attempt to run away like a little baby, eh Gabe? Maybe next time before attempting to flirt with my girlfriend you should take a step back and realize that all she wants is a man. And do you know what Gabe? You're not a man. You're a little shrimp who puts purple highlights in his black weird hippie hair like a little freak. You can't even close your locker without shutting yourself into it. So you know what Gabe?

The next time you even think for a second about flirting with Darla," he leaned in so close that I could see the plaque growing between his teeth, "Well, let's just say you'd better think twice."

And just like that this big self-proclaimed 'man' shoved me into my locker, which I was still attached to thanks to the longest strings ever strung through a mass produced hoodie.

So what if I like putting purple streaks in my hair? Sometimes growing up in a small town really has its benefits, like closed minds. I love those.

I've had the biggest crush on Darla since the fourth grade. I had dibs on her first. No one really thinks about who had first dibs nowadays, do they?

It was Valentine's Day and even though we were only nine, some of the girls had little innocent crushes on some of the boys. If anything it may have not even been a "crush" as much as a boy trading a girl his pudding cup for her gummy bears. And trust me, at least in my mind, anyone who trades his pudding cup for a gummy bear has to be a god on some level.

Anyways, it was Valentine's Day and some of the kids had an extra valentine to give to that special someone that their heart desired. I of course didn't because, well, I was nine. (Hello, I still played with Hot Wheels.)

Darla was passing out her valentines gifts, when she walked over to me, pigtails draped over her shoulders, leaned in and said, "I made sure put two lollipops on your card." Then she winked, and for the first time ever made me turn into a puddle of goo. Before then we'd been strictly friends, but at that moment, I knew I was going to marry her.

In elementary school we always had recess before lunch. One time when we were at recess I caught a caterpillar and put it in my pocket. When I got back to the classroom I wrote a note saying, 'I hope you like our new pet' and put the little guy on it, and placed it on her desk. She got back to the classroom after I did and went to her cubby and grabbed her lunchbox. When she got back to her desk she was talking to her friend and slammed the princess lunchbox on the table so quick, she didn't even realize there was anything there.

I knew he'd been squashed. I stared at my food the whole thirty minutes without looking at anyone. When she was done with lunch, she lifted up her box and found the little guy stuck like putty between the note and her lunchbox. She screamed and I stared at her, half scared and half sad for my little creature.

At the point where we are now, drifted so far apart, I'm probably better off being friends with my own buddies. Actually let's change the plural singular. Buddy. Sounds about right.

Good old Tony.

The day of the caterpillar incident was the day I really knew how strong mine and his friendship was. After Darla had shrieked, our teacher stood up to see what all the commotion was.

After coming over and reading the note, she asked the class, "Who did this?"

"Darla, obviously," Tony told her, pointing to the dead bug.

"That's not what I meant," she said glaring at Tony. "Who brought the caterpillar inside? Everyone knows not to bring little bugs inside. They belong outside on the trees or on the playground. When people bring bugs from nature inside, this is the kind of thing that happens."

All of the kids in class stared around at each other, before the teacher finally spoke up again, "Who brought the caterpillar inside?" Still crickets. "Fine then, if no one can tell me who brought him inside then everyone can have a silent recess tomorrow."

Silent recesses were the worst. Usually they were held on rainy days but sometimes they were given on days when the class had gotten too out of hand. Students had to either read a book or work on homework.

Nobody liked silent recesses.

"I did it," Tony told the teacher while he stared at me.

"Thank you, Tony, for telling the truth. I'm sure the class thanks you as well."

"You're welcome ma'am," Tony said as he sat back down in his seat.

"Not so easy, young man. Come to my desk. I'm going to have to send a note home to your dad."

"What? Why?"

"Because you broke a rule. You brought a bug into the classroom and on top of that you made a big scene at lunch."

"Fine," Tony glared at me the whole time he was standing at the teacher's desk.

That wasn't the only time he'd stood up for me and bailed me out of a Darla issue. It was the first though.

●

I made it through another first day at school.

From the first time I was old enough to walk home from school I've found myself in a habit of stopping by my favorite scenic overlook. Usually I try to pass by it but I become magnetized and have no other option than to sit on the large rock wall and stare out at the open valley. I'm not quite sure what it is about the place but ever since I was a little boy there's been a peaceful serenity about it. Almost as though no matter what was going on in my life I could come here and feel reassured that everything was going to be alright.

We live in a rural area of the Appalachian Mountains. It's so rural that the town we live in is actually called Rural Hall. The little sign that welcomes visitors through it says 'Population 2,001'. I often wonder why they even bothered to add the '1' at the end of the '2,000'. Maybe they thought it would actually add importance to our tiny village if we had one more person living in it. Of course the sign welcomes people to come through it rather than welcome them into it. No one passing through town ever stays unless it's the middle of the night and they're just dying to stay in a little old motel in the middle of nowhere.

Rural Hall is just an old mountain town in the middle of a scenic route. Simply a dot on the map, even though most maps don't even have it marked. We have one high school, one middle school, and one elementary school in town. The middle school and elementary school have even been in debates before about whether they should just combine the two, to cut down on maintenance expenses.

We've lived here all of my life, and my parent's lived here all of theirs before me. My parent's never really had any reason to leave since they'd grown up here all their lives. I really can't say that I'd blame them for sticking around in this little town. The only thing that would've possibly benefited from them uprooting the family to see the world outside their doorstep was that my dad might actually still be alive.

Both of my parents were pressed for money with a toddler running around the house. Food for three is a lot more than food for two, especially when the toddler has to have special goat milk formula. That plus the price of diapers would have anyone scraping the floor for pennies. At least in this town where you either have no money whatsoever or your parents are the mayor or own the local Wiggle Piggle. Of course I can't hate them too much, at least not the owners of the Wiggle Piggle, seeing as how Darla's their daughter. The mayor on the other hand has a huge son named Jake. They could've done without spawning.

A few months after I was born my parents had a heart to heart meeting.

"Sheila, we need to talk," my dad said as he hung up his coat one afternoon after work. He sat down at the little round kitchen table by the front door of our modular house.

My mom had been in the kitchen getting supper ready. "What do we need to talk about?" she asked as she took her apron off and walked over to sit beside him.

"Works going good, you know," he said as he tucked a lock of her blonde hair behind her ear, "but I know you can tell that we're not exactly making ends meet around here. I mean if it weren't for the fact that we have a well we'd probably be scrounging the couch for coins to cover the water bill."

"I already do that for formula."

"I know," dad licked his lips and put his free arm on her shoulder, "I talked to the boss man about picking up third shift. They needed a guy and I told them I was ready and willing."

"Alright, well, that's great. Then you can help out around the house during the day."

"Exactly my thoughts and maybe you should also consider waiting tables again? I mean we really could use the money, Sheila."

I'd heard the same old story over and over from my mom. Whenever I got too out of hand she would remind me of everything they'd laid on the line for me. Why they even had to have me in the first place was beyond me. Why bring a kid into the world if you can barely even afford to support yourself? Seems like common knowledge. Support yourself first and then have kids. They loved each other so much that they wanted me. They tried their hardest to make ends meet and I can't help but respect them for that.

Dad figured that if he spent the next year on night shift that he would have enough money for them to live comfortably for the next few years so that they wouldn't have to worry over money any more.

One evening he had kissed my mom good night and roughed up what little bit of hair I had on my head and went out the door for work. After clocking out he loaded up into his truck and got out on the road.

At five in the morning a 23 year old had just left her boyfriend's house in a rage. They had been drinking and fighting throughout the night and decided right then and there that she was going to end it. She packed all of her belongings into her car and took off in a storm of rage. Unsure of where to go so early in the morning, she decided to just head to a girlfriend's house on the other side of the mountain. She drove half drunk, half hung-over. She came around a bend too fast and hit an old pick-up truck head on. The trucked clipped the side of the overpass, sending it barreling into the valley below.

My dad was in the pick-up truck, that old pick-up truck that had belonged to my granddad. My dad was headed home from work where he busted his butt so that my mom and I could have food on the table. His life had been ended by a selfish girl who couldn't wait till the morning after she'd sobered up to leave her boyfriend.

Maybe it's a little morbid that I enjoy stopping by the overlook that my dad flew off of when I was a toddler. Maybe I find peace here knowing that he died working his rear end off for his family.

# Chapter 2

"GAAAAAAABE!" Yelled Tony as he hurled towards me on his skateboard.

I had gotten up from where I was sitting and tried to make a run for it but was too late.

PHWAAAAM!!! Tony slammed into me, throwing me on the pavement. Another Perkins man hit by someone coming down the hill. Even though Tony was all of ninety pounds and stood in at barely five foot tall he still could pack a punch when flying down a hill on a skateboard.

"Couldn't have given me a little more of a heads up, Tony?"

"I could've, but that would've meant me actually caring."

"And I call you my best friend why?"

Just then Tony grabbed a pack of cigarettes out of his pocket and waved them in front of my face. "Because I'm the only friend you have and the only one willing to risk using my fake I.D. for some ciggs."

"Ah, thanks for reminding me. I knew there was a reason."

He threw me the pack as he plopped down beside me. I lit it up my little deadly savior. My mom despises them. Her dad used to smoke and a lot of good it did for him. So much good that they dug a hole for him to climb into. I'm really just a social smoker. Given the fact that I don't have too many people to be social with it's not that big of a deal. It's not like it's a habit or anything, but occasionally it's nice to let a little steam off. I'm not violent so I can't vent in the way my dear friend Jake might. I'm really a lover, not a fighter. I get a release by sitting by the overlook with the hopes that maybe, just maybe, Tony will drop by to hang out. If he happens to have cigarettes on him, then so be it.

"Made it through the first week of the school year alright?" Tony asked as he flipped his baseball hat around as sweat dripped down his tanned skin. Being Hispanic has its perks. I on the other hand was pale year round.

"Yeah, I just love having first period with the dynamic duo."

"Hah, I'm sure you do, especially since you get to eyeball Darla."

"Oh yeah, let me tell you about it."

"Yikes," Tony took another drag. "So, how's your mom?"

"She's good. They promoted her to manager a month or two ago so she's fine by that."

"About time. How long's she been there? The least they could do is promote her after slaving away ten years."

"Yeah, she's been there long enough. I always told her if I make anything of myself I'm going to take care of her the way she's taken care of me."

"Hah, well if she's promoted to this here managerial job she may not even need your help."

"She wouldn't have to work a day in her life." I stared out at the valley and just thought about the possibility of making it out of this town, "How awesome would that be?"

"As long as you're taking care of me too," he winked and lifted his eyebrow, "then its allllll gravy to me."

I really think that if I had other people to hang out with I'd drop his friendship like a sack of puppies into a river. But then again he has been my wing-man since kindergarten. So I guess I'm obligated to stick with him. And given the fact that he always makes a point to take the blame for me, there's that too.

"Hey man," said Tony, "so I know you're not much on partying but Darla's throwing a shindig tonight since her parents are out of town. I know how much you like the girl so I thought I'd give you the heads up. You know, just in case."

"How do you know about the party?"

"She's got this cute friend who invited me. Dumb as a bag of rocks but she's still pretty cute," he put his hands in front of his chest and made melon shapes.

"Ah, sounds like a must do for you then. Kinda weird that Darla wouldn't say anything about it to me though."

"Not really, I mean it's not like you're in the same crowd or anything."

"Yeah but we're friends."

"Dude," Tony said staring me straight in the eyes. "That girl is not your friend. Maybe eight years ago when we were playing with bugs on the swings she was but the girl is not your friend. She's a girl you like. If she was your friend she wouldn't smother you with her and Jake's relationship."

"Yeah, well maybe she just does it because she knows I like her and is trying to prove something."

"Right. What's she trying to prove?"

He had me. I couldn't think of anything that she'd be trying to prove.

"Exactamundo." Tony looked me over, "Look, just because she's not necessarily your friend it doesn't mean she doesn't like you. She's always had a thing for you. So are you going with me?"

"Tony, her boyfriend could pulverize me into a million smithereens if he wanted to just by looking at me. I'm alright she's not worth the hassle."

"Not worth the hassle!?" He said as he acted like he was going to fall backwards, "Gabe, I'm shocked, like I'm seriously shocked. You're giving up on Daaaaarla? No way do I believe this."

"Well believe it because I'm good."

Was I really good? Hmm…Uhm no. I wasn't good. I was far from good. I wanted to go to the party with Darla, I did. Did I want to put up with the hassle of Jake while being at her party? No. Not one little bit. Nor did I feel like stringing myself along to hang out with Tony and have to wait outside of a bedroom door while he had fun with an airheaded chesty girl.

"Alright, suit yourself. I'm gonna get home and take a shower. Hit me up if you change your mind." He tossed me the pack of cigarettes, flipped his hat around forward and headed back down the road.

As Tony skated off I really had to hold myself back from yelling out that I'd go.

●

Right when I got home I knew my mom was going to smell the smoke from Tony's cigarette (also known as my cigarette) on my clothes. I figured that with it only being four in the afternoon that I'd have enough time to hop in the shower and throw some clothes on before she got home.

But, but did I have enough time to?

"There's my favorite boy!" I heard my mom say as I walked through the door, "Jeez, I've just missed you so much today. Come give me a big bear hug. I could use one after all the insanity at the diner today."

Moms have the best timing in the world.

I leaned in to give her a huge hug when she pulled back from me with disgust.

I could only guess why.

"Good grief, Gabe," she said as she plugged her nose and waved the air in front of her. "You reek. I thought I told you what I thought about those cigarettes."

"Well, I mean it's not like I really smoke. I didn't even smoke a whole one. Just a couple inhales and I was good. I've only had enough in my life to count on my two hands."

She stared at me in disbelief.

"Okay, maybe the fingers on my hands and a couple hands of the people who farm the tobacco."

"Honey they're just not good for you and they're gross. I mean, what would your friend Darla think if she had to kiss you after smoking? It'd be like kissing an ashtray."

"A) I don't really ever smoke and B) you'll never catch me kissing Darla." My mom's shoulders slumped and I threw my hands up in the air, "Darla could fall off the earth for all I care. It's not as though I even exist in her world. She has a man like Jake who has money."

"A man?" My mom said laughing, "He's a fifteen year old boy for Christ's sake. He doesn't have money, his parents do. And what does he know about being a man? You want to see a man? Look at your father. He never wasted money on things like cigarettes and he did his best to put food on the table."

"You see where that got him, mom? He's dead. Dad's dead, and has been dead since I was a toddler." My mom paled and I stayed strong in my theory, "I didn't even really know the guy. How am I supposed to learn from a man that I never knew? How am I supposed to live up to the standards of a dead man?"

My mom pursed her lips at me and threw her hands on her hips. "Listen here mister ungrateful. Your dad was an amazing father figure and was the best man you could've ever had to look up to. Unfortunately all you have are the stories I have from his past. Unfortunately for a boy like Jake his parents are too wealthy to even have to worry about how they'll take care of their son. Jake will never know what it's like to have a parent who busts their butt for them. I wouldn't go looking at a boy like him to be an influence on your own ideals in life."

"But mom," I didn't even have anything else to say. I could see the tears swelling up in her eyes and could see her temples pulsing beneath her skin.

She raised her eyebrow.

I had pushed my mom too far. The best thing to do was to leave her alone. Leave her alone not just because of the fact that I knew she was hurt and I hated to see her that way, but because she'd been hurt at my hand. I may seem like some punk who doesn't give two licks about whether or not I hurt someone but when it comes to my mom I do. She's been a mom and dad for me. She'd be the one to make the dinner and chop the wood for the fire place….in theory. I couldn't imagine having to go through the pain she's gone through. But for one second, just one measly little second, I'd like to come home and not be lectured by that woman.

I took her crazy eyebrows as my queue to go ahead and take a shower. I slammed the door behind me and tore off the smelly clothes. Honestly I hated the smell of cigarettes also. I couldn't stand the way the smell stained my skin even after a shower. Maybe it's genetic that I would despise the smell. When I was done I heard my mom tinkering around in the kitchen. I really didn't want to have to face her. I knew I'd be up for some kind of punishment, and I just wasn't in the mood for being talked down to.

I threw some fresh clothes on and decided maybe that party over at Darla's house wouldn't be such a bad idea. So what if Jake was going to be there? It's not as though I had to be in the same exact room with him the whole time. Who's to even say that I would have to see Darla? It could just be a fun escape that would happen to have free booze. Fortunately we have a one story house, which makes for perfect escape mode. But then again, how many mobile homes do you see out there with two stories?

I grabbed a clean hoodie and jumped out of the window. My skateboard was leaning on the chain-link fence so I picked it up and walked down the gravel path until I reached the paved road where I could ride my skateboard.

It was already about eight by the time I made it around the mountain bend. Tony probably had assumed that I still wasn't going and had probably already left his house to get to the party. I debated whether or not to ride over to Tony's house but I would've had to gone the opposite direction. I didn't want to risk my mom seeing me pass by the front door twice so I just kept riding. I'd just have to meet Tony when he got there.

Darla's parents lived in a huge house on thirty acres. There was a wrought iron gate that would open electronically and had the family name engraved on it. Their driveway was brick rather than the usual cement and wrapped around a circular water fountain that had a little peeing boy standing in the middle of it. Apparently it was supposed to be a replica of the 'Manneken Pis' in Belgium. What is it with rich people and their peeing statues?

When I arrived at the party it was already going in full gear. The door was wide open so I just let myself in. I saw a group of girls that I had some classes with so I went and talked to them for a little while. Seeing as how they were standing beside the drinks I figured I'd kill two birds with one stone.

The prettier one in the group was blonde and voluptuous. They called her Candy. I couldn't help but wonder if this was Tony's friend. I'd remembered seeing her walking out the utility shed at school a few times with random guys.

"So Gabe," started Candy with a hazy voice, "I've been looking all around for Tony and can't seem to find him anywhere. He is coming right? I mean, I was the one who told him he should come in the first place. I thought he would liven up the party a little bit."

Cha-ching. I should've bet money on it.

"Yeah I thought he'd be here already too. He was the one who told me about the party." I looked around at the tall ceilings and the light fixtures, "I really thought he'd be here already."

"Oh that's right," Candy said as she tightened her gaze, "you probably wouldn't have been invited seeing as how Jake kinda has it out for you. Darla probably wouldn't want any problems." She looked me up and down and took a swig of her drink, "Probably why she didn't invite you."

My jaw hit the floor and all of the sudden Darla rushed over, "Candy what is wrong with you?" She took the cup from Candy's hand and poured it out down the nearby sink.

"Well I don't know Darla, I was just talking to Gabe and mentioned that maybe he didn't get invited by you because you didn't want a scene to happen with Jake around and all."

"Well guess what Candy? You just caused a scene." She took me by the hand, "Come on Gabe."

I shrugged and followed Darla into the den where it was quiet and there weren't any people.

She looked around outside of the threshold of the room and turned her attention to me. "I'm super sorry Gabe. I just didn't think that you'd come to the party is all."

I stared at her.

When I didn't give a response she continued, "I know that Jake is kind of a turd. I swear he's just a big fluff ball, he just is so complicated."

"Darla its fine, I mean your fluff ball isn't the kind of person I want to run into again so I think maybe I should just go. He hasn't seen me here yet so it's probably better to keep it that way. I really didn't think I'd run into either of y'all tonight or I wouldn't have come." I gestured at how immense the house was, "I mean seriously this place is huge. I really didn't want to start anything. It was just a good excuse to get out of the house."

"It's no problem. I mean you can stay. Should stay." She hesitated for a minute and thought back to what I'd just said. "Wait. Gabe did you just say again? As in Jake had a run in with you before?"

"No not at all," I hesitated, "well not exactly. He basically told me just to know stop flirting with you. I wasn't aware of the fact that I was flirting with you. I really don't want to cross any friendship boundary or anything. Honestly."

"He didn't hurt you did he? Oh my gosh, like if he hurt you I'm going to be so mad. No joke. You've been my little buddy forever. I swear I'm going to kick his butt for hurting you."

"Darla he didn't hurt me. I swear. He was just being confrontational. Nothing wrong with a little confrontation. And this might sound crazy but a girl your size kicking his butt may not be the best idea."

"Gabe, as God as my witness I'll never let my boyfriend hurt my little buddy ever again," she leaned in staring me dead in the eyes. She took my head in her hands and planted a long wet kiss on my lips.

"I think I'm in heaven," I said.

From the threshold I heard kids making 'ooh' sounds.

Darla and I turned our heads towards the door simultaneously. Jake was standing there. He was way larger than I remembered and was surrounded by nearly everyone in the house.

"Where did they come from?" I asked under my breath as my eyes grew wide.

"Gabe you may want to run," Darla said.

"Oh crap," I said as I dashed out the side door of the den.

"GABE!!!! YOU LITTLE PUNK!!"

He came after me like a puma after a prairie dog. If you ever studied biology you would know that a puma can out run a prairie dog. Not only that but they are above the prairie dog on the food chain, as is Jake above me on the food chain. I tried my best to run but I only made it to the front door, where I tripped and fell. I fell flat on my face. Of course Jake took it upon himself to use this as an opportunity to kick my arse.

"Jake stop!" Darla shouted, "You can't beat up a kid who can't even run away from a beating. I mean he practically just beat himself up from that fall."

"Well he's going to be doing a lot more falling around here."

Jake being all of 250 pounds of muscle and lard, standing at 6'2, picked me off the ground. Me, silly little Gabe, weighing in at a measly 130 at 5'6. It's likely you could already tell what direction this was going, but if not I'll aid in your visual.

Jake, still holding me by shoulders, threw me down off of Darla's porch onto their beautifully manicured lawn. He jumped down off of the side of the porch and started pounding my face. What did I do? I fought back.

…Just kidding.

I actually curled up into a fetal position. Right there in front of all the 'cool' kids from school. I really couldn't care less if they saw. As cliché as it sounds, I just wanted my mommy.

"Holy Crap! Gabe!" Tony shouted as he came running in from the front gate. Of course, given the length of the driveway it felt like it took forever for him to reach me.  When he got to my side he shouted, "Are you seriously in the fetal position? Be a man! Stand up for your woman!"

"TONY!" I shouted, "Why don't you be a man and stand up for your woman? You remember her right? Gabriella!?"

"Everyone stand back!" Tony shouted as he waved his phone in the air, "I have a phone and I know how to use it! Leave the boy alone or I call the cops and have them bust every one of you guys for underage drinking."

"Have it your way," said Jake as he gave me one last blow to the gut before standing up. He went and grabbed my skateboard from the side of the house and looked back, "Is this thing yours?" I guess he could tell from the look in my eyes, because not even a second later he broke it in two without hesitation. Then he just walked away. Scott free.

Tony ran up beside me to help me off the ground. "Dude what was that? I didn't really think that you'd go out and try and beat the guy up. What were you thinking?"

"Walk me home? My luck, crazy will end up chasing after me when Darla's not looking."

"Well I can't just let you walk home alone. With the way you look, you'd make people think there was a zombie apocalypse beginning."

"Is it really that bad?" I hoped he'd say no. Tony's always exaggerating.

"Dude you look like crap. And not in the way you usually do."

We started walking and once we were for sure out of the hearing range of the house and the running range for that matter, I explained my situation.

"Darla kissed me."

Tony stopped in his tracks "Who did what?"

I looked at him for the idiot he was and said in a dumb voice, "Duh-arluh kissed may."

"Well I heard that, but I didn't get the gist of it. So she just kissed you with her big burly man in the other room?"

"Don't just stand there, keep walking."

"Alright now tell me what happened," he said as we continued walking.

"Your date was Candy, right?"

"Yeah, you know Candy?"

"Yeah, she's in a class or two with me. Ohhhhh and she's the reason Jake pounded me in."

"Why is it her fault? I thought you kissed Darla?"

"I did but it began with me talking to Candy near the drinks and she began talking crap about me being there when she remembered that I used to have a thing for Darla."

"Used to?"

"Not the point. Darla stood up for me and found out Jake had been messing with me. She was just so in the moment and passionate about whatever that she kissed me. Low and behold Jake and his crew of goons were all watching."

"That's pretty crazy."

"You're telling me."

"Enjoy explaining your new face to your mom."

Right. My mom. For a split second I forgot I had one of those. One of those lovely women of whom you have to explain your every last detail of life to. How fun this shall be.

Tony's phone started vibrating.

"Candy just texted me and asked me to meet her out in the woods past Darla's house."

I couldn't help but stare at him like he was insane because, well of course he was, "What?"

"Come on, you don't really care, do you?"

"What do you think?"

"Hey look," Tony said as he looked at my bruises and cringed. "You do look rough." He shook the thought away and got back on his train of thought, "Look, it's not Candy's fault that she wasn't born the brightest crayon in the box. Can you really blame me if I want to go have a little fun?"

"No, I guess not."

"Thanks. Hopefully your mom lets you out of the house sometime soon."

Tony took off to have a little Candy.

●

Before stopping off at the house I figured I'd swing by my spot. It's on the way home and it's so beautiful to look out at the valley at night when all the little lights from the houses flicker. Looking at the skateboard in my hands I realized there was no way for me to ride it again, so I threw it in the trash can at the overlook. Then I went and found my favorite part of the rock wall to sit on.

There's this little part just in the middle of the rock wall, where all the rocks are smooth, no jagged edges. As if someone came by and buffed away all of the imperfections. When you sit there and gaze out it makes you feel like you're on top of the world. And after all the crap I'd been through that night, I could have used being on top of the world .

I was sitting there a good ten minutes when a large gust swept through and nearly knocked me off the ledge. Regaining my balance, I adjusted where my butt was planted.

"Well aren't you living on the edge?" asked a voice coming from behind me.

I turned around and in that moment I witnessed the most beautiful person I've ever seen. Darla had been what I thought was beautiful. But I guess in Rural Hall, she's what anyone would have equated to beautiful.

The girl who stood before me had dewy ivory skin and waist length golden hair. Her eyes were the shape of almonds and burned a honey brown. She had a heart shaped face with cheekbones that could cut ice. Her lips, pouty and all, were a fleshy pink.

I couldn't help but be taken aback by her beauty.

"Well, aren't you sneaky," I said when I finally regained some form of consciousness.

"Sorry if I spooked you," she said with a comforting voice. "I just saw you sitting alone and thought you could use some company. Now that I've seen your face I think you could use some medical attention."

"I'm fine, thanks for the concern though. I'm Gabe, I don't think that I caught your name," I said as I extended my hand to shake hers.

"I'm Zipporah, everyone calls me Zippy though."

"What an interesting name."

She nodded, "I know, not many people wandering around with a name like it."

"Your parent's must've been hippies or something, eh?"

"I suppose you could say that. Your name is quite lovely, fitting, really."

"Thank you," I said as I scratched my head. I had no clue whatsoever of the meaning behind my name. I knew it was from the bible, but other than that just assumed it was a regular old name. You know, people name their daughters Rebeccah and their sons David, often regardless of their religion.

"I gotta admit though," I continued, "It's kinda strange having a fairly attractive girl creep up on me. Usually I'm the one doing the creeping."

Zippy looked at me kind of freaked out and then spoke up, "Well I'm sure you're not that creepy, and I wasn't trying to creep up on you, I promise."

"You must be new in town."

"No, I don't live here but I'm not too far from here either."

"Oh so you must be out here with another county's football team for the game?"

"Wrong again. You might want to stop while you're ahead. I don't think you're going to get too far trying to figure me out."

She was very possibly one hundred and ten percent right. I couldn't believe that out of all of the years I lived here, any day this girl could walk up to me, it would been a day like this where I'd been pulverized by a giant, to the point where I looked like some demonic creature.

"So," Zippy said as she took a seat beside me, "what happened to that face of yours?" She paused, smirked, and continued, "I've heard about the mountain lions around here but had no clue they could do so much damage yet let someone get away so easily."

"I wish I had been attacked by a mountain lion. It was more like a bear. A big huge bear."

"Well how'd you manage to get away from that one?"

"Let's just say it was a human the size of a bear. And I'm friends with his girlfriend."

"Ah. How long have you two been friends?"

"Since elementary school."

"Well then what's the problem? I mean, as long as he understands you're just friends and you respect the girl's relationship."

I lifted my eyebrows and turned my attention to the valley below.

"I assume you must've crossed some boundary."

"I'm not so sure it was necessarily me as it was her."

"We all have control over our own actions, Gabe. Even times when it seems like we don't. You like her more than just a friend?"

"I guess. I mean. I always have but I didn't kiss her. She kissed me. And it was more of a pity kiss than anything."

"Well you seem like a smart guy. Keep your head on straight and you'll be just fine." She let out a little huff, "Think about this though. How would you feel if the tables were turned? If you were dating Darla how would you feel if you walked in on her kissing some guy?"

"Pretty crappy I guess." I sat there quiet for a few minutes. "Thanks Zippy." The time donned on me, "Man, my mom's gotta be freaking out. I have to go."

"Oh, alright. It was nice to meet you, Gabe."

"Nice meeting you too. I hope I see you around sometime soon."

"I'm sure that you will."

●

The lights in the house were out as I walked up the gravel driveway. "Please let her be asleep." I mumbled to myself.

I gently opened the front door and poked my head inside. The lights were still off. Thank goodness. I came inside and began walking across the room.

"Nice of you to come home, Gabe."

"Holy crap," I said as I jumped out of my skin. I turned around and could just make out the shape of my mom sitting at the kitchen table staring me down. I couldn't help but wonder if a Cheshire grin was about to appear from midair.

She flicked on the nearby floor lamp. "What in the world," she said as she got up from the table. "Oh my God, Gabe! What happened to you?"

"I went to a party at Darla's house and her boyfriend basically gave me a makeover."

"Well that's some makeover."

"Yeah it wasn't as pleasant as people make them out to be."

"What did you do to make him do this?" She threw her hands up, "It doesn't matter what you did, no one should do this to someone. Isn't he the mayor's boy?" I nodded, "Well, just wait until I give them a piece of my mind."

"Mom please don't, it'll only make things worse."

"How can things possibly get worse around here? You come home reeking of cigarettes, you mouth of to me every chance you get, you just snuck out of the house, and when you finally came home at midnight, you came back bloodied, bruised, and beaten by some jerk at your school. I'm just about fed up with your crap, Gabe. If you can't straighten up I'm going to have to take serious action."

"What's there to do?"

She cocked her head to the side, "What's there to do? How about a strict to and from school only policy? How about a no video game policy? Oh even better and get this, I like this one the most. A no Tony for a lifetime policy?"

"I'm really sorry mom," I said as I looked at my feet.

"Well as sorry as you are you still have a lot of thinking to do. Look at me when I talk to you," I looked up and she continued, "Fortunately for you, you look so horrible that I'm not even worried about grounding you. I think somehow or another the universe has paid you back for the havoc you've been wreaking around here. I'm not even in the mood to punish you. We're going to go to the doctor's office first thing in the morning to make sure you're one hundred percent okay."

"Yes ma'am."

"Go to sleep. Now."

As I headed off to bed she called out to me.

"Oh, Gabe..."

"Yes?"

"Straighten up."

"Okay."

●

Nine o'clock came too fast.

My mom rapped on the door with her fist repeatedly to wake me up.

"Get up, throw some clothes on, and come to the kitchen. I have some breakfast on the table but we have to be at the doctor's office in an hour."

I threw the covers off of my body and dragged my feet to the dresser. After opening the top drawer where my boxers were I found it empty. As I scratched my head I did a scan around the room. In the corner I spotted a pair of plaid yellow boxers. I walked over and checked the insides out and gave them a whiff. Clean.

Saturday morning breakfast included pancakes. Today they were shaped into hearts which was almost horrifying. She only makes heart pancakes for special occasions. And seeing as how I could win the worst son of the year award right about now the special occasion must be the marking of me being grounded for life.

I crawled into the dining room chair and my mom came over and put a few pancakes on my plate.

"Eat quickly," she said.

"Yes ma'am," I said as I reached for the syrup and smothered them to the point they were gooey globs. I saw her staring at me and I couldn't help but notice her aging. She was still thin and attractive in the face but was beginning to get wrinkles around her eyes. It made me wonder if this had just happened overnight from the torment I gave her yesterday or if she'd been aging all along and I just never thought much to stare at her.

A stream of syrup dribbled down the corner of my mouth. I grabbed my glass of juice and used the edge to scrape the remnants off my face and licked the high fructose corn syrup off the cup.

"You do see the napkins in front of you, right?" she asked.

"Yeah, there are napkins aren't there?"

My mom lifted her eyebrows and nodded.

When I was done I ran to the bathroom to brush my teeth. I shot myself a glance in the mirror and couldn't help but realize that I looked like the guy from The Goonies. My left eye was bruised and swollen and I had a huge gash between my chin and jaw. I knew that I'd been feeling like I was hit by a car but I didn't think it actually looked like I was.

My mom and I left the house, jumped in the car, and hit the road. As we turned around the corner on my favorite bend I saw my overlook, the most beautiful place in my world. There in my spot (MY spot) was a girl with a long ponytail looking out over the valley. As I looked closer the girl turned around. It was Zippy. I waved to her.

My mom looked at me and then in the rear view mirror, "What're you doing?"

"The girl that was on the ledge. I met her last night. I was on the way back home from the party and met her at the overlook."

"Hm, maybe it's not such a good idea to meet a girl when you look the way you do."

"Huh?"

"Not such a good first impression. Might scare her off."

"Thanks."

"I'm just saying you waved and I looked up and there wasn't anyone there. Might've freaked her out."

"What are you talking about? She was just there."

"Like I said, you may want to wait until you get doctored up a little before trying to pick up more girls."

"Maybe you just didn't see her because you were driving. Jake would've seen her out there. He could spot a girl a mile away."

"Speaking of Jake…"

I threw my hands up in the air, "Oh God mom. Please tell me you didn't say anything."

"Gabe, look in the mirror. Can you not see how bad you look? That boy attacked you, for no reason but hormones. I mean, son, you're black and blue all over."

"What's black and blue and red all over?"

"It's not funny. It's really not. So I called his parents up. I went to school with his mom; Mary Lisgnet was her maiden name. I was even good friends with her when we were kids and then when we got to high school she realized that if she wanted to get anywhere she had to get in with the 'in' crowd. Well she did and when she did, she stopped talking to me. I guess my parents didn't make enough money anymore for her to want to stick around. Then again she did get married to the town mayor so I guess she has all of her life accomplishments racked up."

"Mom get to the chase. What did you tell her?"

"I just told her what any mom would say in the situation." She let out a big sigh, "She didn't seem to believe that her perfect little boy would hurt anyone that bad. Apparently she had a chat with him and he said he was only 'playing around'. Darla happened to be over having breakfast with them and piped up. She told his mom how bad he roughed you up."

"Darla actually said something bad about Jake to his own mom? Man, that's a bit of a sellout."

"Well be glad she sold him out. Mrs. Jenkins offered to pay for any doctor bills that stem from him beating you up, as long as we don't go to the newspaper about it. Perks of getting beat up by the mayor's kid."

"Wonderful, now I get to feel the wrath of Jake at school on Monday. How awesome."

Mom looked at me and tilted her sunglasses down, "If he even takes one step near you I'll not only be calling his parents but I'll also be getting a restraining order on that crazy kid."

●

Everything in the hospital room was white. Not paper white but white with a tinge of yellow. I wouldn't call it off-white because it was more of a sickening shade. Similar to the shade of a white plastic Lego after it's been around ten years. The halls and rooms smelled of bleach fumes. As if they knew the hospital was old and dingy but they still wanted some fraction of you to believe they were keeping it clean and up to date.

"So you had a run-in with good old Jake Jenkins, eh?" Dr. Weiss asked when he walked through the door.

"Something like that," I responded.

"Well I'm not surprised. A star on the high school football team with a temper the size of Russia, paired with wealthy parents." He made a 'tsk-tsk' sound. "That is just a cocktail for disaster. They think they're God's gift to Earth and that they're invincible."

"What about Gabe?" Mom asked, "Nothing wrong? He hasn't been acting weird but he did wave to a girl on the side of the road and I swear I didn't see her. He's also been a major pain in my rear lately. Could he have some kind of concussion?" Dr. Weiss opened his mouth to talk and my mom cut him off, "Or maybe just the idiot portion of his brain is flared up?"

"Mom the girl was there. I swear I saw her just as clearly as I'm seeing you right now."

"Hm," said Dr. Weiss, "Maybe we should have a CT scan done. Most likely nothing's wrong. But we just want to make sure he didn't have a concussion from the incident."

"Alright, well when do we do that?"

"We'll go ahead and get it taken care of today."

At the doctors and my mom's request, I did the CT Scan. Doctor Weiss told us to go ahead and head home that they'd let us know something within the next day or so but that we shouldn't expect anything. So that's exactly what I did. I didn't expect anything.

●

Luckily for me, my mom had work on Sunday. So who was to know whether I was sitting around the house not getting into trouble, like I should've been? That's right, no one. I took it upon myself to skate on over to Tony's house to play some video games. After a couple hours of staring mindlessly into a TV screen I was pretty worn out with it.

"Why don't we get out of here and go skate around. Maybe float into town and go to the arcade."

"Hey Gabe, why don't we not do that? I just got this game a couple days ago and haven't gotten to play it. Why don't we get through a couple more levels and then we can get out and skate? Why skate to an arcade when we've got a brand spankin' new video game right in front of us?"

"Meh. I dunno. Fresh air, maybe?"

"Since when do you care about fresh air?" He gestured to the TV, "We've been staring into that black hole for years and never wanted to leave it for this 'fresh air' you speak of."

"Maybe I got punched too hard in the head or something but I'm just not in the mood to stare at a T.V. for hours on end. I think I'm gonna head out."

"Alright bro. Well you do what you do. I'll catch up with ya in a little while."

"Cool. I'm gonna make a peanut butter and jelly sandwich before I go, alright?"

"Hah have at it. If there is any."

He knew his house better than I did. There wasn't any. At least not any jelly. Tony's mom left town when he was a kid and abandoned him with his dad. Quite the bachelor pad, it was. For Rural Hall that is. Since they were out of jelly I had to go on a conquest to find something else to use in place of it. If I used peanut butter on its own my mouth would become glued together.

I opened a few cabinets. Ketchup. No. Soy sauce. Definitely no. There it was, tucked away in the corner of the cabinet. Pancake syrup. I'm pretty sure I heard angels humming when I stumbled upon it. I actually sometimes preferred a peanut butter and syrup to a peanut butter and jelly anyway.

I rolled out with my sandwich in hand and Tony's old skateboard underneath my feet. Since Jake broke mine in two, Tony went into his dad's shed and found a skateboard he used when he was younger. He had gotten a new one last year for Christmas and gave me the old one. Once again it was Tony to the rescue.

I swear this town may not be the wealthiest but the aesthetics of the place really makes up for it. Skating up to the overlook I finished off the rest of my sandwich and plopped down to just observe Mother Nature at her finest.

"You have a little peanut butter in the corner of your mouth."

I'd know that sweet voice anywhere. I looked beside me and found that it was no one other than Zippy.

"Hey you," I said as I licked the peanut butter from the corner of my mouth.

"Peanut butter and jelly sandwiches are my favorite," Zippy said.

"Yeah I'm pretty fond of them too except this time around it wasn't peanut butter and jelly but a peanut butter and syrup."

"Oh wow. Sounds like an…interesting combination. Whatever floats your boat I guess?"

"Yeah," I patted the spot beside me, inviting her to sit down.

"So how ya feeling newspaper boy?" she asked as she joined me.

"Huh?"

"You know, what's black and white and read all over?" Then she let out this huge guttural laugh.

"You're funny. But not the first one who's ever said that one. In fact, I was telling my mom that joke yesterday. I think you have it a bit wrong though."

"Oh, do I?"

"Yes, in my case I'm pretty sure it would be black and blue and kicked all over."

"I think you're version hits the nail on its head."

"Speaking of driving by you this yesterday, my mom like totally freaked when she saw me wave to you."

"Why?"

"Well for starters she got on this spiel about the way I look and how that's not a good first impression."

"She might have something there. Fortunately for you the bruises can't hide your cute face."

I blushed, "Ah yeah. Well and then she looked in the rear view mirror and didn't see you. She was convinced that either you ran away in fear when I waved or that I had gotten a concussion and was seeing imaginary beautiful girls."

"So how'd the whole doctor's office thing go? You all A-OK?"

"Yeah I'm good. They did a CT scan just in case."

"Oh."

Just then I saw what looked like a cloud of concern wash over her face. "Don't be getting all upset. It's just because I got beat up some massive kid on a steroid rush. I mean I'm perfectly fine. I may not look it from all the crazy marks on my body but trust me it was just in case I had a concussion."

"Oh I gotcha. You know, I was thinking about your mom. Maybe it's best that you don't mention anything about me to her."

"Why? I think talking about someone other than Darla makes things a little bit better."

"I'm just thinking, you know, with the whole Darla thing and the situation you're in with Jake maybe it's best not to throw another hat in the ring. Of course I want to be your friend and all. But I just think that if anything your mom shouldn't have to worry about another girl with a crazy boyfriend."

"Ah, of course someone as pretty as you would have a boyfriend."

"Nah I don't really do the dating thing. I'm just saying that from your mom's perspective she may not be too thrilled about another pretty girl who could have a crazy possessive boyfriend."

"Ah, so you think you're pretty huh?"

"I didn't say that. You did."

"Oh I guess you're right." I felt my cheeks redden, not because I was sitting next to a pretty girl but because she knew that I thought she was a pretty girl.

The valley pulled my attention away from her. I watched a birdy fly up from the town below. As it passed overhead I saw Tony barreling down the hill on his skateboard. Once again straight in my direction only this time I had my beautiful friend with me.

"Zippy watch out!" I shouted towards her so she wouldn't have to be a part of the pile up but whenever I went to help her off the ledge she wasn't there. She must've taken off when I was staring off into la-la land.

"Who're you yelling at crazy boy?" Tony asked.

"My friend Zippy. She took off when she saw you hurdling towards us."

"Not my fault if your girlfriend can't handle you're wild other half."

"Nice of you to decide to join me."

"Eh. You were right. I needed to get out of the house. I was starting to look around and see dots on the ceiling."

"Don't you have popcorn ceiling?"

"Yeah, but they were shiny little dots."

"Gotcha."

"So who's this girl?"

"Zippy. Remember the other night when you abandoned your best friend to get meet up in the woods with Candy?"

"Vaguely," he said as he diverted his attention to a nearby bush.

"Well thank gahd you did because I stopped up here and she creeped up on me."

"Cool. See I knew some good would come out of you having to walk home alone. Just imagine you may not have met her if I was there with you. No girl in her right mind goes up to two guys in the dark when she's all alone."

"Yeah I guess. I like her she's pretty cool."

"Then get with that."

"Yeahhhh," I said staring at him, "She's sweet but I'm not really trying to get into any relationship. I think I'll be celibate like a monk."

"If it's because of Darla, she was a different story. You were trying to get with a girl who already had a guy dipping into her cookie jar. Zippy on the other hand…"

"I don't really see her that way. Besides I'm way too out of her league. She's not the kind of girl you want to date because if anything ever bad happens you wouldn't be able to talk to her again."

"Gotcha. She sounds pretty cool. Don't let her jet off next time without saying 'hey' to your best friend."

# Chapter 3

It was Monday morning. First period, with Jake. AWESOME.

Not really though.

I was sitting in my seat with the hood of my hoodie covering my head in hopes that I could hide from Jake.

"WELL, well, well." Ah the sound of Jake in the morning, "If it isn't my little buddy, Gabe." He walked over to my desk and nudged me on the shoulder.

I swear I just wanted to curl up into a ball and die. Just die.

"Don't worry little Gabe. I won't hurt you…again." He leaned down and peered underneath my hood, and our eyes were only inches apart. He began to whisper as spit flew out of his mouth when he talked, "At least not while my parents are paying your medical bills."

"They're only paying for what you did."

He stood back and grew louder, "It's OK not everyone can be a tough enough man to not go running to his mommy and daddy every time they get hurt. Oh wait," he said as he cocked his head to the side, "I guess you would just be running to your mommy."

"Are you kidding me? Are you that much of a tool that you want to make fun of me because my dad died? Grow up." I shoved past him and tore out of the classroom and down the hall to the bathroom to recover from my emotions. I stared into the mirror for about ten minutes before I heard the door open.

"What do you want Jake!?" I spun around towards the door and saw Darla. "Darla I really don't think now's a good time. Honestly I don't think it's ever going to be a good time. So how about you just get out of the bathroom, leave me alone, and never talk to me again."

"I'm sorry, Gabe. I just was going to come tell you that," she hesitated and continued, "I'm sorry. I broke up with Jake. I didn't realize how mean he was until he started saying all that stuff about your dad."

"What? You're just as insane as he is. You didn't realize he was mean when he bashed my head in on Friday night?"

"I thought he was just being jealous."

"Just being jealous? Are you kidding me?" I looked her up and down in disgust, "You're nuts. You deserve to be with him. He's been a jerk his whole life and you're just too naïve to see it."

I stepped back and thought a minute, "You know what Darla? You're just as reckless as he is."

"What're you talking about?"

"You're so selfish that you get caught up in a moment and kiss someone, not thinking about how people are going to be affected. Do you not think that your boyfriend or ex-boyfriend, or whatever you're calling him this morning, do you not think that he's going to try to come after me again? Especially now that you've made it clear that you're following me to apologize?"

Darla was still standing near the front of the bathroom, speechless. She darted her eyes around to the urinals and the stalls. I couldn't tell if it was my anger or the sweet musky smell of the bathroom that was making her eyes tear up.

"Your idiot boyfriend beat the crap out of me. Then after beating me up he came to school and started talking crap about my dead dad," I looked at her ready for her to run out crying but she didn't. "And on another note you're not a boy, so why are you even in here in the boy's bathroom? Are you nuts?" I threw my hands up in the air and they fell back to my side. "Oh wait, of course you are."

"I thought you just went down the hall." She used the back of her hand to pat away the dampness under her eyes. Adjusting her shirt, she continued, "Right after you ran out the door the office called over the intercom that your mom was here to pick you up. Mr. B had me come after you to let you know. And you ended up in here. So I came in here after waiting by the door for about ten minutes. So I'm sorry for what Jake did to you and I'm sorry for following you."

"Well thanks for coming in here to tell me my mom was here but no thanks for your apologies. You can keep that along with your crappy boyfriend."

"Ex-boyfriend."

"I really don't care anymore Darla," I said as I shoved past her.

●

I walked into the school's front office and saw my mom sitting in a chair looking frazzled.

"Hey mom, what's up?"

"The doctor called and said that I needed to bring you down there ASAP. Apparently something came up on the CT scan."

"Like what a concussion? Wouldn't I be out cold?"

"I'm not sure, Gabe. They really didn't say much. Just that it was serious and that he needed us to come down to his office immediately."

We left the school and hopped in the car.

"Mom, what do you think is going on?"

"Honey I really don't know. I don't really want to talk about anything until we get there. There's no sense in getting worked up about anything if we don't know what's going on."

"Yeah I guess you're right."

"I am."

We sat in silence for a good ten minutes. She looked over at me and asked, "How was school?"

"More like first period? It sucked. It sucked big time. King Jake and his queen were there. I wish they hadn't been but they were."

"Did he mess with you?"

"Usually when I pair the term 'first period sucking', with the name 'Jake', there's a possibility that he's the reason that it sucked."

"You have to be kidding me?"

"Nope."

"I am going to be having another chat with his mom and I'll also be going by your school and asking that he be removed from any of the classes that y'all share together. He needs to leave you the alone and they need to know that their little football star is going around terrorizing kids." She gazed out the window for a minute before returning to me. "You should probably leave Darla alone too."

"No problem. I have no interest in her whatsoever." She stared at me in disbelief. "No joke. I had been in the bathroom when the front office called over the intercom about you being there and she had to come hunt me down. I basically went off on her. It's ridiculous. She just doesn't even care how her actions impact other people."

Mom lifted her eyes at me, "Aha, is that so?" I rolled my eyes. "So what happened with Jake?"

"He just got all in my face and started talking about dad."

"What?" She looked at me with the same pain in her eyes that I had in mine not even an hour ago.

"Yeah exactly and then I left the class."

"I'm really sorry, Gabe. I really am."

●

We entered the waiting room and walked up to the window at Dr. Weiss' office.

"Hi can I help you?" asked the clerk behind the window.

"I'm Sheila Perkins, Gabe Perkins' mom. Doctor Weiss called us about a CT scan Gabe had done on Saturday and asked us to come in as soon as possible."

"Oh, Ms. Perkins, Dr. Weiss mentioned you'd be coming in. If you just have a seat I'll go ahead and check you in. The doctor will be out shortly."

We had a seat and waited. Dr. Weiss came out to greet us promptly. He walked us back to a room and took the x-ray out of his folder. "Ms. Perkins," he said to my mom and switched his attention to me, "Gabe, I called you two up here for a serious matter." He clipped the x-ray to the board and turned the light on. "Upon further inspection of your CT scan we noticed a strange shape, a fried-egg type shape, if you will."

"Dr. Weiss, I already had breakfast and I'm not in that big of a mood for craps and giggles. What's wrong with me?" I asked him.

"Gabe," he said rubbing his cheek, "we believe we may have found a tumor."

My mom let out a gasp, "What do you mean a tumor?"

"Ms. Perkins, we have found what we believe to be a tumor in your son's temporal lobe. It could explain his seeing the girl that he waved to if in fact it is a tumor."

"She's a real girl and must've moved after I waved to her. No explanation needed."

"What do you mean by if in fact it is a tumor?" My mom asked, "Is there a chance that it's not? Is it a tumor or isn't it?"

"Well," Dr. Weiss said, "We're pretty sure it's a tumor Ms. Perkins, however we need to do a biopsy to make sure of whether or not it's malignant or benign. If it is malignant the biopsy will help us know the extremity of it. We also need to do a biopsy to know what kind of tumor it may be."

"This is just so all of the sudden." Mom patted down the crease in her pants, "Well, when do we do the biopsy?"

"We'd want to go ahead and do it as soon as possible. If you look at the X-Ray you'll see that it looks as though the tumor is located on the outer edge of the temporal lobe of the brain." He said, encircling the shape with a dry erase marker. "Because of this we may not have to open up his skull to do the biopsy."

"You're going to open up my skull?" I felt a wave come over me and I felt as though all of my organs were about to exit via my mouth. They practically did as I puked all over the floor. I stared at the vomit for a good thirty seconds, "I thought the puking didn't start till chemo?" I darted glances between the two looking for an ease in tension.

"It may if you need it," said Dr. Weiss. "You won't have to go through chemo unless it's malignant and even then there are other options. We really just need to focus on what we're dealing with one step at a time. Now we're going to try and do the biopsy just with a needle. Our neurosurgeon would drill a small hole in your skull near the tumor and then the needle will be inserted into the hole and a very small minute piece of the brain tissue from the tumor will be extracted. We'll then test the tissue to find out what kind of cancer it may be as well as what grade it might be at. "I've already talked to one of the best neurosurgeons in the region and he said he'd clear his schedule for you any day next week."

My mom sat there in shock. Seemingly more shock than I was in. The last few days have made me somewhat numb to any pain I could endure, emotional or physical.

"Sure, next Monday should work fine," she said.

"I'll get in touch with him," Dr. Weiss concluded as he left the room.

"C is for cancer, that's good enough for me" I sung in a low voice, mimicking the character I watched on T.V. throughout my childhood, as I sat on the ledge of the overlook.

"I'm pretty sure that's not how it goes," said Zippy.

"That's how it goes for me these days."

"These days? Gabe, you've only known about your tumor for six days. You sound like an old man who's had the gout for about twenty five years."

"Ahhhh the gout. If only I just had the gout."

"I'm just trying to cheer you up. You know, I really like cheering you up."

"It seems like that's your purpose in my life. I mean you did show up right after I had my rear end kicked to California and back."

"Maybe God just crossed our paths so I could be your picker upper."

"Hah. Good one. God."

"Why do you say it like that?" She leaned back and just stared at me, daring me to talk.

"Like what? Like oh yeah there's a God looking out for me. I get my butt kicked one night by one of the scariest people I've ever seen then the next Monday the same guy gets in my face again and not even three hours later I find out cancer. Oh yes Zippy. There SURELY must be a God."

"If there's not a God then explain to me how it's possible that you just happened to get your butt kicked to the point where you needed a CT scan? And on that CT scan you found out you had a tumor?"

"I call it sheer coincidence. I call it, I would've found out that I had this stupid thing at some point and it just happened that I found out now versus two years from now."

"Who's to say you would've been around two years from now?"

"Yowza." She was right. I might not have been around two years from now. "Wow Zip. You're just freakin' awesome, you know that? For a girl who usually knows how to be a picker-upper, you really just did your best work right there."

"Gabe, I'm not trying to hurt you, I'm just saying," she paused looking for words. "I'm just saying…Gabe, be grateful for what you have now. So you have a tumor? Others have had them too okay?"

"So I'm ungrateful now?"

"Don't get it twisted, okay?"

"I think I should go."

I got up to leave and she shouted, "Gabe, come on!"

Still walking away I continued the conversation, "No, Zippy. I have to be up early for my biopsy anyways. I'll see ya round."

"Good luck," she said as she bit her bottom lip.

"Thanks," I said heading up the hill.

●

It was five a.m. on a Monday morning and I had already been up for an hour and a half. I couldn't believe that I was sitting in a hospital bed with a dress on waiting to have some doctor drill a hole into my head. It sounds more like some horror film than any reality I could've ever imagined. I'm fifteen for crap's sake. Fifteen years old and I have a tumor. Hi I'm Gabe. I have a brain tumor.

Perfect pick up line eh? I think so.

"Hi Gabe, I'm Florence but you can call me Flo," said a heavyset black woman with such long eyelashes that they looked like spiders were crawling out of her eye sockets. "I'm going to be your nurse, and in about ten minutes I'm going to wheel you out to surgery. Is there anything you need that I can get you?"

"I need you to get rid of this tumor for me. That's really all I need."

"Honey," She said as she leaned down over me, "I know this isn't what you expected to have to go through when you turned fifteen but I also know you're a handsome young man who has a lifetime ahead of you. Our neurosurgeon is an amazing one and we're going to make sure that we can do everything to help you. God is looking out for you," she reached out and held my hand in hers and gripped me tightly, "And so is Nurse Flo." She dropped my hand and winked as she left.

67

Why is it that all of the sudden, because I have a tumor that people keep talking about God? I mean is it because of the tumor itself? As if just because I have a tumor everyone else freaks out and feels the immediate need to enlist a religion upon me? Or the fact that tumors are often deadly and they'd rather have peace with themselves knowing that they could give me some sort of false hope?

Nurse Flo came back in, "Ready hotshot?"

"As I'll ever be."

"Alright then let's get this show on the road," she said as she came around behind my bed and began to wheel me off to the O.R.

When I got there the neurosurgeon I'd talked with was there, along with about five other people dressed in white. "How's it going buddy?"

"I'm a boy in a dress with no underwear on. Does that give you some sort of idea?"

"I see," he chuckled.

The anesthesiologist came around and put an octopus mask on my face and I breathed in the magical air of the anesthesia fairies.

●

"Welcome back to the world handsome," I heard Nurse Flo say as I looked around the blurry room.

I looked over at her groggily, "Hi ma'am."

"Well look who's awake," said my mom as she walked over to my bedside. "I've been waiting to talk to you."

"What about?" I asked.

"I really don't know. You being in surgery all that time just made me miss you. I just," she looked down at her hands and back at me. "I just love you."

"Now," Nurse Flo said as she moved between the monitor near my bed and my bedside, "you still have your catheter in so no funny movements till I take it out in a little while."

"Well why can't I take the creepy thing out now?" I asked, realizing the strange feeling of the device.

"Because we just want to make sure that you're able to get up and move before taking it out."

"You mean I won't be able to get up to pee?"

"The cool thing about it is you don't even need to get up to go pee."

I looked down beside my bed and saw a little baggy filled with urine, "Oh, that's just disgusting."

"We all get one at some point or another. I'll be back in a little while to see how you're doing." She began to leave the room and turned back, "by the way, honey, you have a visitor outside."

My mom looked over at me and asked, "Do you think you're up to seeing anyone? You just woke up?"

"I'll be fine mom. I'm sure it's probably just Tony anyways."

"Ah. All the better." My mom pressed the red button on the wall to intercom the nurse's desk. "Hi, I'm Sheila Perkins, in room 208. We were told that there was a visitor for my son and we wanted to let them know that we're ready for them."

"Yes ma'am," said the voice on the other end of the speaker. "I'll send her in."

"Her?" I mumbled.

My mom just shrugged.

The door creaked open and Darla slid in. Time for a face palm. After six years of the biggest crush on earth I would've never thought I would've dreaded seeing her.

"Hi Gabe," she said hesitantly from the doorway.

"Darla what is it going to take to get it through your thick skull...."

"Well, I'm not here to see you Gabe," she cut me off as she turned her attention to my mom, "Ms. Perkins, would you mind if I talked with you for a few minutes?"

My mom looked at Darla and back at me. "I don't see why not."

They started to leave the room together.

"Mom are you kidding me?" I said as I rolled my eyes in the direction of the window.

She lifted her hand to me in response and left the room with Darla.

I was clueless as to why Darla came to my hospital room in the first place. How the heck she even knew I was in here is beyond me. I hadn't told anyone about me having to get this stupid biopsy done. I hadn't even told anyone about the tumor other than Tony. I really don't see Tony being the one to tell Darla though. He's not in the same three ring circus.

Regardless as to why she stopped by, I was getting tired. Maybe because it's around 6pm and I'd been up since 3:30. Or maybe it's because I just had some guy drill a hole into my head.

●

"Peekaboo," ahhh, the sweet voice of the angels.

I peeled my eyes open and saw Zippy.

"Hey," I said groggily. "How long have you been here?"

"Not too long, just a little minute."

"Cool. I wouldn't have wanted you waiting around here while I was just sleeping. Could've got boring."

"I wouldn't have minded. Honest. How ya feeling?"

"Not too shabby. Like someone drilled a hole in my head."

"Can't be that bad?"

"Nah. Darla stopped by, that's probably been the worst of it."

"I know I saw her when I was passing through the hospital. She was in a family waiting room with your mom."

"Oh really? You didn't happen to overhear anything did you?"

"I didn't really stop to eavesdrop. Your mom was just crying and hugging her."

"I'm sorry. I don't know why she won't leave me alone. I've tried to tell her I'm just not interested anymore."

"You don't have to explain to me, Gabe. I'm just your friend."

"You know, I wouldn't mind if you were more than just a friend."

"Like I said, I'm not big on relationships. I'm big on friendships."

"Yeah, yeah."

"Anyways, I just wanted to check in on my little buddy. I'm sure your mom will be coming back any minute now. Take it easy for me, alright?"

"Sure thing, Zip."

"See ya 'round," she said as she waved goodbye.

Right after she walked out of the door my mom walked into the room. "That was Zippy, mom."

"Huh? That was Darla."

"No, the other girl. The one you just passed in the hall."

She just stared at me confused, "You must've just woken up from a deep dream. Coming off anesthesia will do that."

"Mom, the girl you just saw coming out of my room. She's the girl that I saw waving to me at the overlook who you thought wasn't real. Her name's Zippy." I looked at her for affirmation but she remained looking clueless. "Her name's Zippy and she just walked out of the room right as you were walking into it."

"Gabe, you're confusing me. There wasn't a girl."

"Maybe you just weren't paying attention."

"I dunno hun, but I'm going to have find out from the nurse what meds they have you takin."

"Anyways," I continued, "what did Darla have to say?"

"Well," she sat on the edge of my bed, "first let me start of by saying that she really does care about you. That she considers you a great friend of hers and even though some bad things came from being friends with her, I think you should give the poor girl a second chance."

"Really? Just the other day you were saying I should probably keep my distance from that crazy."

"I know but I think you should give your friend another chance."

"Why? Did you not see what her nutso boyfriend did to me? I mean what if even though she broke up with him he still comes after me because he thinks I made him break up with her?"

"I know that you have a bad taste in your mouth about it but just try. Apparently, since Jake's parents were paying for the medical bill they found out about the tumor."

"How? I had no intention of telling anyone what was going on. I didn't want anyone to treat me any different than they had. I mean I just don't want sympathy friends. I'd rather them keep treating me like crap until I die. Then maybe they'd revisit how they treat people after I was dead."

"Jake's parents somehow had gotten the bill from the appointment after the CT scan and Mrs. Jenkins inquired about why she needed to pay for another appointment after the initial one that dealt with the bruises. Even though she wasn't listed as someone to give information to one of the medical technicians at billing is new and assumed that since she was paying for the visit that she had permission to tell her. Mrs. Jenkins had called and talked to me about everything. She wanted to help pay for your procedures. Seeing as how I don't exactly make much and we aren't on insurance I let her."

"Are you kidding me? So now I'm basically endowed to Jake. He's going to make me his slave around school now. He must've told Darla." My mom nodded her head, "Well this all freaking sucks. So I get that Darla now knows about everything but why would she be here? And why would she want to talk to you?"

"Aside from the fact that I'm quite the interesting person," she said with her eyebrows up in the air, "she wanted to talk to me about you. If in fact this tumor is malignant, you're going to have to go through things like chemotherapy and have to have a lot of doctor visits. So knowing that her ex-boyfriend's parents were going to do some of the funding for you, she asked her parents if they would as well. I went to school with her parents as well. They own the local Wiggle Piggle in our town and some others. They decided that they'd set up a donation fund for you."

"That's what Darla came to talk to you about?"

"That's what she came to talk to me about."

Maybe I had been too hard on Darla. If she could look past the fact that I went off on her at school maybe I could look past the fact that she indirectly got me beat up. "Oh, well I guess I could try to deal with her as long as her shadow isn't following her around."

"Yeah that might not be such a bad idea. And as for Jake, I really don't see him being a problem anymore."

Funny how things change when people find out you have a tumor.

●

A day later and I was still stuck in the hospital bed. They wanted me to stay just in case there were any complications from anything. Fortunately there weren't any. Even if there were could there really be anything worse they could tell me?

About nine a.m. I packed my things up and got my clothes on. Dr. Weiss was scheduled to drop by and let us know the results of the biopsy.

"Knock, Knock." Said Dr. Weiss as he opened the door.

Why people announce themselves with 'Knock, Knock', is beyond me. Either say 'hello' or knock on the door. Don't verbalize the action. It renders the physicality useless.

"Dr. Weiss, how are you?" My mom asked as she extended her hand.

"I'm great thanks," he said as he reached his hand out to meet hers.

They shook hands and my mom sat back down beside me on my bed.

"We had a look at the biopsy and it doesn't look that great."

"What does that mean?" I asked, "I have a tumor so I didn't expect it to look 'great' but something is either great or not how can something be 'that' great? Like I'm kinda on the verge of freaking out."

My mom grabbed my hand, "It's going to be OK."

"The situation we have on our hands is a serious one." Dr. Weiss said as he pushed his glasses back up his nose. "From the biopsy we found out that your tumor is actually a malignant one, which means that it is cancerous. We did some testing on it and have found out that you have an anaplastic ogligodendroglioma tumor. As much as I hate to tell you this, you're tumor is at a high grade."

"So what does this all mean?" Mom asked, "Gabe is only a fifteen year old boy? How could he possibly be so bad off with us going so long without knowing?"

"Well," Dr. Weiss continued, "Although ogligodendroglioma occur mostly in older men, about six percent occur in infants and children. Sadly, the growth of these types of tumors is generally slow so they could be present for years before they are even diagnosed. However one of the symptoms, aside from seizures and headaches, is personality changes, which you had spoken with me about, Ms. Perkins. I'm sure that alone wouldn't have been enough for a cancer diagnosis as Gabe is a pubescent teenager and most teenagers give their parents a hard time while they grow into themselves."

My mom nodded her head.

"I'll continue," he said. "Given the fact that this tumor is in the temporal lobe, it makes it even more silent, rarely causing any more symptoms other than possibly seizures or maybe even perhaps language troubles and since he'd never had either of those issues there was no need for an inspection."

"So you're basically saying that he could've been living with this tumor for years and we just never knew."

"Precisely."

Still sitting in shock I let the adults continue.

"So where do we take things from here?"

"From here I would suggest we try chemotherapy. Because of how aggressive the tumor is we would want to start immediately."

"What about school? Would he still be able to attend his classes?"

"As long as Gabe feels up to it he could definitely continue to go to school. In fact I personally would recommend it because it would give him something to focus on rather than the cancer. Chemo can however, take a lot out of a person. So if for some reason he feels too weak at some point to go, I'd definitely give him the option to stay home. But other than that all he'd need to be careful of were the germs simply because the procedures to fight cancer weaken your immune system."

I finally decided to pipe up. "So basically what you're telling me is I have an extremely aggressive case of brain cancer." I waited for a nod from the doctor, "You've told me 'yadda yadda' this and 'yadda yadda' that about getting better. But what you haven't told me is if you actually think it's going to help. If I sit through days of radiation and chemo am I actually going to get better? Or am I just going to feel like a turd as I speed towards death? Because if the latter is the case then count me out. If you actually think I have a chance then sure but I would much rather die happy than die over the course of two months miserably."

Tears began dripping from my mom's eyes.

"Gabe," said Dr. Weiss, "I think you're a young man who potentially has a lot of time left ahead of you. How much? I don't know. If I gave you an exact estimation, that's all it would be, estimation." He cracked his knuckles and looked from the paperwork to me. "And I don't want to lie to you. I can't sit here and say 'Yes you're going to live a long healthy life', just as I can't sit here and say 'You're going to die', because I don't know. I'm not God. I'm a doctor and though I want to help you, I can only help you as much as God and science gives me the ability to."

"Thanks. That really helps." Not. Once again I'm stuck not only worrying about whether or not I'm going to die. But now I've also heard for the umpteenth time about God. And this time not just from a beautiful girl or a spirited southern nurse but from a doctor. A doctor who should have all of his faith wrapped up in the theory of evolution and scientific happenings. Doctors usually have science based beliefs. Give me something factual that I can actually see some statistics on. Not some shallow hope in a God.

# Chapter 4

It was three weeks since I started chemotherapy. I never thought how important my hair would be to me until a lame Thursday.

It had been raining all morning and finally when the rain had subsided I decided to crawl out of bed. Even though it had been raining I wanted to go out to the overlook. On rainy days after rain stops pouring, steam drifts up from the valley below. It's one of the most beautiful sights a human being can witness. Any time it happens I always have the tune rush into my head, 'Smoooooke on the waterrrr', even though it's the valley. My mom raised me on good music, what can I say? I digress.

I hadn't seen Zippy since the hospital, and chances are if I was sitting there she'll pop out behind a bush and creep up on me. She's such a breath fresh air and after lying around the house for the past two weeks I really could've used some.

So I went to the kitchen and poured some cereal into a bowl. It was the good kind, full of sugary goodness that turns to mush if you let it sit in the milk too long.

I hadn't been to school I a couple of weeks. Blame it on the chemo. About five minutes after starting to eat I felt the hurling sensation coming on and jetted off to the bathroom. After puking my brains out, I realized if I was going to go see my Zippy I was going to need a shower. Who wants to be friends with someone who reeks of stomach acid and bile? Not me.

While I was in the shower I started lathering my hair with shampoo. I always enjoyed having a big mass of bubbles lathered up on top of my head and couldn't help but despise any shampoo without sodium laurel sulfate. Natural shampoos just never give me the right amount of lather. Not having enough lather is a sin, I tell you. SIN.

As I was rinsing out the shampoo I happened to grab a huge clump of my hair from my head. I didn't think I was massaging my scalp that hard.

"Dang," I mumbled. "Maybe it is time to switch to all natural shampoos. This stuff is toxic." That's when it hit me. My hair was starting to fall out. All the oxygen in my lungs slammed out of my body. The hair fell from my hand, and I finished rinsing out the shampoo and climbed out of the shower.

I looked into my mirror and noticed how patchy my hair looked. Now I'm not sure if it was because my hair had fallen out of the shower or if it was just the fact that it was the first time I had actually looked at myself in the mirror in a good few weeks but I saw what I had been trying to ignore. Ignoring what I knew was bound to happen. My face wasn't the same full, baby fat face I had gone into my sophomore year with. My face had become angular. I was beginning to resemble a Central American cow during dry season. Frail and bony.

I threw my hoodie and some jeans on and raced out the door. I didn't even bother drying my hair since the heat probably would have made the rest fall out anyway.

I was waiting at a stop sign at a busy intersection and looked across the road. Zippy.

"No, no no," I mumbled. Why did she have to choose today to find me somewhere other than the overlook?

She was walking across the road towards me and I began speed walking like women in the wealthy neighborhoods. Running would make it too obvious that I'd seen her. Speed walking would just mean that I'm some crazy person who walks fast.

"Gabe!" she shouted.

I kept going, trying my best to avoid her. She was the last person I wanted to see. Two hours before she had been the reason for me to crawl out of bed but in that moment I couldn't even face her.

"Gabe, wait up!" she shouted again.

I stopped in my path and just stared at the ground. I was too weak to keep speed walking. Even if I did I knew I would eventually slow down and she would catch up with me. I turned around and just stared at her.

"What's wrong with you?" Zippy asked.

"What's wrong with me? What's wrong with you?" Aren't I clever?

"I was just shouting your name and you wouldn't slow down but you just kept going."

"Zippy look, I'm not really in the mood to see you." I paused for her to get the message, "You're the last person I want to see right now."

"Why?" she saddened and stepped back, "I'm sorry, did I do something wrong?"

I could see the pain bubbling behind her eyes, "No you didn't do anything wrong, you're perfect and I just wasn't expecting to see you right now. I woke up wanting to see you but right now, in this moment, I don't want to see you."

"Gabe, what's going on?" she asked as her eyes narrowed.

"You want to know what's going on Zippy?" She nodded, "You really want to know what's going on? I have third stage cancer. I've been taking chemo for three weeks. I feel like a turd that someone dropped on the side of the road after eating greasy Mexican food when they couldn't find a close gas station. I want to just curl up into a ball and never wake up again. Look at my hair." I took off my hood to reveal the luscious locks of cancer. "Look at my hair Zippy. It's falling out in clumps and there's nothing that I can do about it. I look like a goober. And the worst part about it Zippy…"

Just then I saw Tony out of the corner of my eye. The great timing never ceased with that guy.

He ran over to me and threw the hood of my jacket back over my head, "Dude, what are you doing?" He looked around at the passengers in cars staring out the windows as they passed through the intersection, "You must really be having a meltdown."

"I'm having a meltdown? I'M having a meltdown?" I shook him off of me and threw my body up and down, "I have cancer, Tony. I'm fifteen years old and I've got a brain tumor that will probably end up killing me and I'm having a meltdown?" He stared and I shouted, "I think I may be entitled to having a meltdown."

"Yeah man that's cool." He patted me on the back, nudged me toward the drug store, and we began walking, "It's not like it's your fault you got it. And come on now, you may have cancer but you don't have to go around sporting that crazy looking hair-do. Let's go get you a razor and buzz that crap off."

"Yeah, alright. Whatever."

We started walking away and it was only when we had entered the store that I realized that Zippy wasn't with us. I was in such a frazzle that I didn't even stop to introduce her to Tony. That girl has a knack for disappearing. I felt like crap. She must've run off right after he came up to us. Now not only am I a crazy cancer ridden freak with patchy hair but I'm also a jerk who scares off some of the only friends I have.

Tony found the electric razor on the other aisle and brought it to the checkout counter.

"That it?" asked the pudgy bald clerk staring at us as if we belonged to another planet.

"Yeah," answered Tony, "my crazy buddy here has cancer."

I glared at him.

"Why's he crazy?" he said eyeballing me as he wrung up the razor.

"Oh you didn't hear him out there yelling at himself? Never mind. Just was going to break the ice."

"I was not yelling to myself! Zippy was standing out there with me and I went off on her. She was right there when you showed up, don't you remember?"

"Dude I know I've never met your new girlfriend but right now I can't help but think she's a figment of your imagination. Or some person you've came up with so you can make everyone think you're crazy."

"Listen to your buddy," the clerk said to me, "I heard the whole thing and had to eavesdrop a little since you were scaring my customers away out there. I don't remember seeing a gir., just a little boy who looked like he belonged in an insane asylum."

"You two must be nuts. Like, she was right there. Come on Tony."

We left and headed off to Tony's house. In the bathroom we laid out an old towel to collect any pieces that fell on the floor.

"You ready for this?" he asked me.

"Yeah."

"You sure? I mean. You want to cut it all off, right? You've got some of the nicest man hair in school." An idea hit him, "Hey we could always leave like a little rat tail in the back. You know, the rest will be bald and shiny, but then you could have a little piece that you braid. You'd look like a total badass."

"What?"

"Alright, off with it all."

I leaned my head over the sink and Tony shaved away. Ten minutes later and it was down to a stubble.

"Man," I said as I looked in the mirror. "It's still fuzzy."

Tony thought for a second, "Hang on. I know just the trick." He fled out of the bathroom and came back with a razor blade."

"Oh no. Don't think you're going to be coming near me with that thing."

"It's the only way to give you a sleek and shiny look. Trust me."

"Tony, I've already had one hole drilled in my head this month. You better be real careful with that thing."

"I'll let you do mine too."

"What?"

"I can't let you be the only guy around town looking like he belongs in the Arian Nation."

"Yowza. Is that what I really look like?"

He stared at his little razor blade, "You will after this thing."

"Not really the look I was going for."

"Yeah, well. Welcome to cancer my little friend."

I never thought I'd have hair that was shorter than my ears. So far I'd made my impression of creativity throughout high school with my jet black hair with various colored highlights. Now I'm a baldy.

●

My mom got home around six that night. As she walked in the door I couldn't help but wonder what she'd think when she saw my bald head so I pulled my hood up over my head and plopped down onto the couch hoping I could avoid her having to see it. The longer she saw me as normal, the better.

"How was your day?" she asked as she put her keys on the bird shaped key hook.

"It was good."

"Anything happen that was….interesting?"

"Not really."

"Oh." She fiddled around in the kitchen before continuing, "Well I dropped by the drug store on the way home. Thought I'd get some ice cream. I know how much you love Rocky Road. Thought that maybe if you couldn't keep anything down you'd at least be able to savor the flavor of something delicious."

"Thanks I'll get some in a little while." I said keeping my head turned towards the T.V.

"You know, while I was there I saw Jake's parents."

"Awesome. Just what I wanted to talk about," I fell over sideways and laid my head on the arm of the couch as I kicked my feet up beside me.

"Give me a minute before you freak out on me. Well, I was talking to them about some things with the funding and I guess the clerk had overheard me say the word 'chemo' and he piped up. Not too many folks in town, you get one kid who has cancer and just about the whole town finds out about it. He mentioned something about seeing two young guys buying an electric razor. One told him that the other had cancer."

"Maybe someone else in town has the big 'C' other than me. Must be in the water."

"Ahhh, sure. He said that one of them had been shouting to himself outside the store for about five minutes before coming inside with his friend."

"How interesting."

She walked over to the couch and kneeled on the floor in front of me, "You don't have to be short with me. Or try and hide that you shaved your head. I figured you were bound to shave it off after seeing how gapped your hair was getting. I'm your mom. I know when things are going on. You don't have to hide things from me."

I sat up straight and took my hoodie off and just stared at her.

She let out a big sigh and pulled me in to her embrace. She sat back up, pulled away from the hug and stared into my eyes like she was searching for something.

"Honey, I'm worried about you."

"I'm worried about myself too. But I mean as far as the cancer goes we're doing everything we can do. Not like I can shake my head around a little and slap some sense into my brain and say 'RELEASE THE TUMOR'."

"It's not just the cancer that I'm worried about, Gabe. Why were you yelling at yourself outside of the drug store?"

"For the millionth time I wasn't yelling to myself. I was talking to Zippy. I was getting frustrated and I didn't want her to see my hair the way it was so I just went off on her. I went off on one of my only real friends. And then Tony walked up and I guess she just split before Tony could say anything."

"Ah."

"She was there. I saw her. I've seen her here and there for the past month and a half. Ever since that jerk Jake punched the cancer into my head I've seen her."

"Gabe you know Jake had nothing to do with the cancer. For all we know the cancer could've been there for years. It just happened that he was the reason for us going and getting your CT scan done. For all we know it could've been a blessing in disguise." She stopped and stared at me, "But this Zippy girl."

"What about her mom? You haven't met her so how are you going to judge her?"

"Gabe, I'm not judging her. What I'm judging is your mental state."

"My mental state?"

"Has anyone other than you met this girl?"

And that's when it hit me that I've been friends with this beautiful girl for the past two months yet no one has even met her yet. Not Tony, not my mom, not anyone from school.

"But mom, she goes to another school."

"Gabe, the closest high school is 30 miles away. Don't you find it a little bit odd that this girl you see, who by the way disappears exactly when people come around you, happens to be from a school 30 miles away?"

"I never gave it much thought but I know who she is. I know her. She's Zippy."

"Gabe, maybe we should talk more about this with your doctor."

"There's nothing to talk about! She's real and I know she is. Just because she hasn't graced you or Tony or anyone else with her presence, it doesn't mean she's not real!"

I took off to my room and shut the door behind me. I mean I know I'm literally sick in the head. But only from the brain tumor though. I know for a fact that I'm not someone who belongs in the looney bin. I see Zippy and she's as real to me as my mom is.

I needed to find her.

●

Fortunately for me the number one place I like to go also happens to also be the number one place where I can find Zippy. I hopped out of the window in my bedroom and walked down the gravel driveway. The skateboard would've been quicker but I just didn't feel the energy to skate there. Dragging my feet seemed like the best method.

When I finally got to the overlook I hopped onto my favorite spot on the ledge and just looked out into the open. Ten minutes passed by. I figured she'd be sitting beside me by then but she wasn't.

"Come on Zippy. Where are you?" I asked myself as I looked around.

When I turned around I saw her standing behind me.

"There you are," I got up from the ledge and frantically started getting diarrhea of the mouth, "I came down here to talk to you. Everyone thinks I'm going crazy. My mom, Tony, even people I don't know like the guy from the drug store. It's driving me nuts. It's not even just the chemo that's making people treat me different. They all think I'm seeing things."

"I'm sorry to hear that." She hesitated and continue, "And I'm sorry about earlier, Gabe. I know you're going through a lot and I should've just left you alone."

"No it's fine. I'm kind of crazy if you haven't heard."

"I don't think you're crazy. Just sick is all."

"Zippy there's something I need to talk to you about."

"OK." She sat down on the ledge, "Come sit down with me."

I joined her on the ledge.

"What is it?" she asked.

"Well, something strange seems to be going on."

"Gabe."

I cut her off. I needed to tell her what I was dealing with, "No one believes me when I tell them I've talked to you."

"Gabe."

I tried to talk over her again, "In fact no one even believes that you exist."

"Gabe!"

"Why're you yelling?"

"Gabe, I keep trying to interrupt you but you won't stop."

"Well that's because I'm not that big on interruptions. Especially when I'm trying to figure something out and you're the one who need to help me figure it out. So let me finish talking, plea…."

She placed her index finger on my mouth, "You might want to let me interrupt," she said as she took my hand.

"Fine have at it, please, explain to me why it is that everyone thinks I'm crazy when I talk to them about you. Or why you disappear right before anyone comes around. Or why it is that no one saw you when I was yelling at you earlier. Everyone thinks I'm insane after I've talked to you."

"Gabe. I need you to understand something about me."

"What's that?"

"I'm an angel," she said as she looked me dead in the eyes.

I laughed, "I mean, Zippy, you're gorgeous and all but an angel? Really? OK just tell me the truth. You have some social phobia right? What is it?"

"I just told you."

"You think I'm nuts too?"

"No, I never said that."

"Oh, great so you really are just a figment of my imagination. Just like everyone's been thinking. Is it the tumor? The tumor is making me see you, right? I should've known it. I should've known that I'd never have someone as amazing as you be my friend by choice. I should've known that you weren't real."

"I am real though, Gabe." She stared at me with eyes of steel, "Gabe, I've been sent here to be with you through this hard time in your life. Haven't you been wondering why people keep throwing out the possibility of God? Why he's been coming up in conversations far more now than he

94

ever has? He's trying to get through to you. He wants you to see him for what he is. He wants you to know his name."

"His name? What the heck, God's name is God. There I know it. I don't believe this. Zippy you've become my best friend. And now you're telling me you're an angel and that's why people can't see you? I don't believe this for a second," I stood up and rubbed my smooth bald head, "Holy crap my mind really is playing games on me."

I stormed off. I walked all the way home and didn't even look back. What would I have been looking back on anyway? Some self-proclaimed angel girl? I didn't even believe in angels. Why would my mind create such garbage? My tumor couldn't have created some gorgeous Pocahontas woman or some science fiction goddess in steam punk clothing? That would have been amazing. Instead I created some stupid girl who looks like a human but says she's an angel.

I wish she would've said she was a ghost. Yeah, a ghost girl named Zippy. That would've been much cooler. A cancer ridden freak falls in love for a ghost girl. It's like a perfect movie plot. Hell, that would've been ten times more believable, especially for my stupid subconscious to create.

●

I woke up the next morning to the smell of someone making breakfast. Usually I would consider it an amazing smell. The smell of, dare I say it, angels slaving away in the kitchen. Given the circumstances though, I knew I was bound to puke up anything I stuffed in my face so I thought it a good idea to not even think of the way it smelled.

I looked at the clock and saw that it was eleven am.

"Mom?" I asked as I made my way out of my room. "Why are you still home?" She should've been at work by then. Why would she have stayed home from work to cook breakfast?

"Oh, crap," I said, "What did the doctor call and say this time. I only have a week to live, don't I?"

I rounded the corner and saw no one else but my best friend and my ex crush. Tony was sitting on the couch watching the T.V. and Darla was playing Betty Crocker. She even had the whole get up, with the apron and oven mitt.

"God, I hope not. I was hoping I'd have longer than a week to play house with you," Darla said from the kitchen.

"It's about time you woke up." Tony said as he tossed me the remote. "It's all yours, bro man."

"Thanks. What's she doing here?" I nodded towards Darla.

"'She'," Darla started, "Is cooking you breakfast."

"Well that's a nice gesture and all but A) I can't keep anything down and B) I told you to leave me alone. Why won't you just leave me alone?"

"Hm, well A) Tony asked me to come make breakfast for you because he knows he can't cook if his life depended on it and B) I don't care if you want me to leave you alone. I'm your friend and you can deal with it. Now," she said with the biggest, slightly schizo, smile, "Who's ready for some bacon and French toast?"

"Sounds like a recipe for disaster," I said, thinking only of how it would look if it were regurgitated.

"I already figured that," said Tony. "Which is why I brought you some of this," he tossed me a little bag of weed.

"Tony, what are you thinking?" I threw the bag back at him.

"I was thinking my friend has turned into a bag of bones and that he needed my help."

"I've never been high and I'm not going to be now. I mean I'm already dying are you trying to get me in the grave faster?"

"No, but I do know that you can't eat worth a crap. If all you do is throw up everything you eat you're going to kill yourself, you little bulimic." Tony stood up and walked over to me, "Just do it," he said as he pressed the bag into my chest.

"My mom would bust a nut."

"Let her. If anything she'd be glad to see you eat again."

"Well, we can't do it in here."

"Well you can't do it sitting outside on the front porch watching the Po Po's go by. Take it to your bathroom and open a window."

"You say so. If this doesn't work don't even think about bringing this or anything else illegal over to my house."

"Trust me. It'll work," he said smirking.

An hour later Darla was finished with everything and I had the appetite of a lion that had been caged for days in an abandoned zoo. I ate so much that I thought I was going to burst at the seams. I was a teenage boy and growing and all. I needed to grub out on occasion. Thank God for Tony.

"So," Darla asked. "I heard you have a girlfriend now," she said while pushing food around her plate with her fork.

"Nothing of the sorts," I retorted. "Apparently she's just a figment of my imagination." I stared up into space, "Ughhh, a gorgeous figment of my imagination. It totally sucks. The one girl who was gorgeous and had an interest in me is totally nonexistent." I rolled my eyes and my head fell into my hands as I drifted into a day dream.

"Good grief, what did you give him, Tony?" Darla asked.

"Kid's never smoked before, it must have really got to him."

"What're you guys talking about? Darla this….is amazing," my eyes rolled back in my head

98

as I lingered over the delicious crunchiness of the smoky bacon.

"This is hilarious," Tony said.

"Yeah, so back to your figment of imagination," Darla said, "Tell us about her."

"You really want to size up his hallucination, Darla?" Tony asked

"That's not what I'm doing. I'm just trying to get him back into some sort of train of thought is all."

"Righhhhht."

"OH, she's just gorgeous, Darla. Like, I always thought you were beautiful," Darla began blushing. "But this girl, man I saw her and it was like holy crap. It was like," my eyes grew wide and it hit me, "holy crap guys, I should've known this girl was an angel all along, like she was so ethereal."

"Ethereal? What does that even mean?" Tony asked.

"It means not of this earth like all glowy and dewy and crap," Darla said getting annoyed.

"She just had this aura about her. Every time I was around her, I was warm and felt safe. She has this long gorgeous wavy blonde hippie hair."

"Hippie hair? Like the stuff you used to have?" Tony asked.

"No, man, it was this long beautiful hippie hair. Like all she had to do was wash it and it would dry and just become beautiful on its own. The kind of hair you could put flowers in and they'd just stay." I turned my attention to Darla who was just staring angrily at me, "I mean, don't get me wrong, Darla, you're amazing too. You're hair's nice and straight but flowers would probably fall out of your hair when you move."

"She sounds like a cavewoman," she said.

"She's an angel," I shrugged, "What do you expect? You really shouldn't try to compare yourself to an angel, Darla. You're as pretty as earth creatures get."

"You sound insane," she said.

"What can I say? Maybe I am."

"Or," Tony jumped in as he stood up to put his plate away, "You're just as high as a kite."

"I dunno, Tony. I feel pretty normal."

"Trust me, dude. You're far from normal."

"So do you actually believe that you saw the angel? Or do you think the doctors are right about the whole hallucination thing?" Darla said as she eyeballed me.

"Yeah, honestly I have no clue. I'm so confused. I totally thought she was real and was ready to stand up for her against the doctor and my mom but when she told me that she was an angel, I didn't know what to think." I started to stand up and felt weightless, "Woah."

Tony ran back over and sat me down in my seat, "Hang on a second space cadet."

"I just think, you know, that for her to tell me she was an 'angel', it was kind of my brains way of breaking the bad news to me that she was just a hallucination."

"That's crazy that a tumor could create something so superficial like and make it seem real."

"Oh, she was real. Just no one saw her, you know. Like a person in the fog. Really weird. I guess because of the tumor being in the temporal lobe of my brain it can cause me to have hallucinations."

"Hmm," said Tony, "Natural hallucinations. Sign me up."

"And the cancer that comes along with it? You can take mine."

"Good one."

After eating Tony had to run off. Apparently he had skipped a few of his classes to come over. His teachers were already threatening him with failing and when his dad found out he threatened to send him off to his grandparents' house so they could keep a closer eye on him. Tony definitely wouldn't want to go live with his grandparents. They both ran their own private practice together and were shrinks. He wouldn't want anyone keeping a closer eye on him much less a pair of analytical therapists. I assumed that after he left Darla would be leaving as well. But nevertheless I was wrong about that.

"Darla, this food is awesome."

"I know," she said still wallowing in annoyance.

"Look, I know you're mad at me for saying my angel friend was prettier than you. But since she wasn't real she really wasn't prettier than you. You don't have to be mad."

"You really think I'm mad about that?"

"Oh, I don't think you are. I know you are."

"Yeah, I'm SO caught up in something as skin deep as looks that I completely overlooked how much of a turd you've been to me lately."

"Darla, you're nuts. Get this, we were close friends in elementary school but ever since middle school you've been totally blowing me off. Like, no joke, crazy girl."

"I still talked to you at school every now and then."

"Oh yeah and you somehow managed to make sure that it was always when your body guard was around you. Never more than a wave usually."

"You can't blame me though. I mean, everyone goes their separate ways as they grow up. I mean people change."

"I didn't."

"You did, though. And our situations changed. It was normal in elementary school to be friends with everyone. Kids don't see each other for what they have or if they're a girl or a boy. As you get older you have to."

"Oh sorry, apparently I didn't get the memo."

"It would've been hell for me if I didn't start dating Jake when I had the opportunity to. He would've made my life hell. You know that?"

"Really? A pretty girl like you would have a problem?"

"He did it to other girls. Practically started making people pick on them if they didn't like him to some degree. At least in middle school. I mean and if I broke up with him, it would've left me with no standing ground whatsoever. I'm not a cheerleader, so I don't have that to make me popular."

"Wow Darla. I didn't really think you were so caught up in all of that stuff. Really makes me rethink everything I ever thought about you."

I stood up and went to the kitchen to clean up.

Darla slapped her head in her hands and shouted, "I was, ok? She walked over to me in the kitchen, "But that was before everything started happening with you."

"What, my cancer?"

"Not even just that, when Jake beat you up. It made me realize that none of this stuff means anything. High school politics are just that. High school. So what? You've been friendly with me since we were kids, you know? You were always a friend to me. And I tried to give that up for popularity. It's so dumb."

I walked over to where she was standing at the counter and hopped up and sat there on it beside her. "It's not dumb." I thought that through for a minute, "Okay it's pretty dumb but it's not your fault. Everyone in high school gets caught up in that crap. Not just you. And I'm sorry, I know I shouldn't have acted the way I acted towards you. Even though you never gave me the time of day much anymore, you still tried to be friendly on occasion."

"It's fine, you don't have to explain anything to me. I mean after everything, I'm just glad that we're still cool."

"No problem."

"So," she said, looking for a way to change the route of the conversation.

"So, I know that your parents and Jake's parents are funding for my treatments."

"Oh," she hesitated and looked away, "I didn't know that you knew that."

"Well I do and you really don't have to pretend to be all friendly with me and stuff just because your parents are helping out. Their help is really enough. You're not obligated or anything."

"Gabe, I don't feel obligated. I want to be around you. In fact I'm kinda glad that Tony asked me to come over to make you breakfast."

"Really?"

"Yeah, really." She stared at me with her eyes of clover, "You're a pretty cute bald kid."

Suddenly an urge come over me. And for once it wasn't the urge to puke. I had to kiss her. I had to kiss her then and there. I've been waiting six years to kiss her beautiful face. And now was my chance. A real kiss. So I did. Full on kiss. I leaned over the mere inches separating us and kissed her.

Just as my lips slipped past hers, I lost my balance and fell off of the countertop. "Crap."

Darla covered her mouth to hide her laughing, "Oh, my gosh, are you ok?"

"Yeah, I'm fine."

"You tasted like bacon."

"Jeeze, I taste like bacon and I fall flat on my butt."

"It's alright," she said as she got down to my level and stared into my eyes, "I like bacon. It seems to make everything better somehow." She reached up and rubbed my head. "I should probably go."

"I'll be so lonely, though," I said as I pouted my lips.

"I know but Tony's not the only one who skipped class. I'll check up on ya later, OK?"

"Sure. Thanks Darla."

"No problem, cutie. Think you can make it to the couch without me?"

"I guess," I stood up and brushed my pajama pants off.

"Alright, well get some rest, you look tired," she said as she kissed my cheek. "Want me to call you later?"

I nodded, "Yeah, I'd like that."

"Okay, I'll find my way out."

As she walked out of the front door, I flung myself on the couch and passed out in a daze.

●

"Aren't you cute when you sleep?" shouted the voice of a girl who was a figment of my imagination.

"Sorry Zip." I told her, without even bothering to open my eyes, "I'm not talking to you."

"Why's that?"

"Because, old friend, you are not real. If I talk to you after knowing you're an imaginary friend, then I'm basically giving in to my disease. Letting it have its way with me."

"Uh-huh….."

"But then on the flip side if I don't talk to you then I'm still somewhat in control over my own brain." I opened my eyes and finally looked at her.

"Ahhh, I see," she said as she pulled herself off the wood paneled wall and gracefully walked over toward the chair beside me. She pulled up the skirt of her long flowy faded blue and cream dress and puffed it out as she sat down with her feet underneath her. "So this is about you having control?"

I looked at her debating whether or not to give in to the conversation. I tried to wave her off, but she continued.

"I assume you feel as though you have no control in your life, so rather than go on some mysterious ride of giving thought to the possibility of your 'hallucination' being a reality, you'd rather write it off as just that. A hallucination?"

"Not sure where you're going with this."

"Would that really make you feel in control, Gabe? And if so, is it really that controllable? Your situation, that is? You have a tumor. If you could rid yourself of it on your own, wouldn't you have done so already?"

"Zip, you're not real, so if I keep talking to you I'm only making my imagination delve deeper into lies. And I'm good. Go find some other cancer ridden teen to freak out." I pulled the hoodie over my head and flipped over to my right side, facing the couch cushions.

Instantly I saw Zippy's eyes peeking over the couch. I looked back at the chair she was just in, and back to where she was standing.

"What the…"

"If I'm not real why can't you block me out?"

"Because my tumor is obviously killing me."

"Oh, I don't know if I'd go as far as to say that, my little bald friend." She rubbed my head as if she was rubbing a wish out of a genie lamp. "How can I go freak some other kid out if I'm just a figment of your imagination? Wouldn't it only be possible if I were real? To place my attention from one real boy with real cancer, to another real boy with real cancer?"

"Not sure. Don't care." I rubbed my eyes and scratched my head. What the hell did Tony make me smoke?

"I think you do care. Why else would you still be talking to me if you didn't care?"

"Zippy, I'm just fed up with the fact that when I finally met someone cool and down to earth and seriously gorgeous, she ends up being a self-proclaimed 'angel'. AKA non-existent. It's prophetic, really. Did I create you subconsciously to make myself feel like I had a girlfriend? You know, I already have a tumor and who wants to die never been kissed?"

She slumped her head in one hand and used the other to hold her weight as she leaned herself against the couch.

"It's odd though," I continued, "That you'd be here right now, if that's what's going on. I mean I just kissed Darla and it seems as though if you were just a subconscious creation to fill the void of a love interest I wouldn't have made you appear here and now."

She looked at me offended.

"Oh. Well, I guess you would've found out at some point. Me and Darla may just be a thing now. Sorry if that disappoints you, Zippy, or should I say," leaning in, "brain….

Zippy let out a grunt and flung herself over the back of the couch and landed in a cross legged position at my feet.

"No offense, Gabe, but I was never interested in you like that. You're an amazing friend, yes, but I…"

"…Have no intention of having a 'relationship'," I finished her sentence. "I know. How could I forget?"

"All I meant was that I'm not hanging around you so that I can be your girlfriend."

"Isn't that the sole purpose why girls hang out with guys?"

She lifted her eyebrow at me.

"Ah, but then of course you're not a girl." I saw her smirk, as to hint a 'win'. "You're not an angel either missy. You are a hallucination."

"But, what if I'm not? What if, I'm really an angel, here to help you out?"

"Oh angel, rid me of this tumor. Please, I beggeth of you." I rubbed my face, "Can't you just leave me alone? If you are real, is my life not miserable enough that I have to have some angel girl follow me around? Some shadow of death, reminding me constantly why she's hanging out?"

"Maybe it's not just some angel girl following you around?"

"What's that supposed to mean?" I asked, as I lifted myself up in my spot on the couch.

"Maybe there's a bigger picture you should be looking at."

"Like what?"

She rolled her eyes and stared at me.

I caught her drift, "Oh like God?"

She nodded.

"The 'God' who sent you to me? As if some higher power is watching out for me?"

"Yeah. Maybe you should get your eyes off of what's going on in your head, literally and figuratively speaking, and get your eyes on what should be in your heart."

"I'm pretty sure that the cancer is what I should have my focus on."

"Not necessarily. What about what happens after the cancer?

"I've got cancer Zippy. Let me break it down to you creepy girl. If there was a God I'm pretty sure he wouldn't be giving me cancer. And if there was a God I wouldn't have had the girl I've been crushing for eons finally give in to her equally as large love for me but only now that I have cancer."

"Well, maybe that's a God thing too. Maybe you should be thanking God that you've got a chance to be here. It could be a lot worse. You're getting help."

"Zippy, how could it be worse?"

"You could have cancer and have no one even bothering to deal with your pity party."

"I'm not throwing myself a pity party. In case you haven't noticed my cancer is pretty hardcore."

"Sounds like a pity party to me," she said as she crossed her arms. "So what? You're still alive? So what if you have cancer? There are people walking around who are perfectly fine, no critical diseases or illnesses and they'll be walking across the street to get a donut and some coffee, when WHAM, they're hit by a car speeding around a corner. DOA."

I looked at this crazy girl in front of me. Do remind me to look both ways the next time I venture out for some donuts.

"There are people right now," she said pointing down with her index finger to emphasize the time, "Inside of a gas station on the way home from work who happen to stop in right before a thug robs the place and they'll be shot dead for their wallet. There are moms out there who have had perfectly fine pregnancies who will go into labor in the middle of the night only to die giving birth to their babies that they've waited nine months to meet."

My jaw fell open.

"So who cares if you have cancer? You're alive and breathing. You have a chance to make a change in the world."

"Ohhhhh kay miss crazy pants. I think our visit is done for the day."

"Come on, Gabe. Think about it."

"Yeah, well I'm fifteen. What do you really expect me to do to make a change in the world?"

"The biggest change in the world that you can make is a change within your own heart."

"Ah, I think I understand. Right about now I have this feeling that a change needs to be made right now."

Her face lit up, "See, I knew you'd know where I'm going with this."

"Yes. And that change is for you to leave me alone."

"Maybe," she said as she stood up and walked over to the entertainment center where the T.V. was standing. She rifled through a few drawers and found something. "Aha!" she shouted as she turned on her heels toward me and slung a book at me. "Or maybe you could pick this up and do a little investigation."

"I didn't think angels could pick up items from the real world. You know, your hands would pass right through them," I winked at her.

She put her hands on her hips and licked her lips, "Yeah, I ah, didn't realize figments of the imagination or hallucinations as you like to call them, could either."

I swallowed the slobber that was collecting in my mouth.

"What is this?" I lifted the book towards the dim yellow lighting and looked closer. My hands drifted past the leather cover of the heavy text, I opened a page and saw 'Holy Bible' scrawled across the interior in gold calligraphy. "How'd you know where this thing was?"

Zippy shrugged and headed for the front door, "Call it instinct."

"I call it creepy," I shouted her direction.

"Pick it up sometime. It may help you out with some things you're battling," she said lingering in the doorway.

"We'll see. I've got a lot on my plate at the minute."

"Oh yeah, Gabe," she said as she threw her hair behind her shoulder. "Lying around your house all day must be soooo difficult. While you're lying around why don't you give God a chance? Or at least give some thought to that book in your hand?"

She walked out the front door and let it close loudly behind her. I jumped up and ran to the front door. Looking outside I couldn't help but hope she was still out there but by the time I'd gone out to get her she was gone. I was really getting fed up with this amazing imagination of mine.

●

I rubbed my eyes with the backs of my hands and rolled over to glance at the clock.

Five p.m. Mom would be coming home soon. Was I still high? Holy crap, how was I supposed to know if I was sober or if I wasn't sober? Does a stoned person know if they're stoned? Or is it only the people around them that can tell?

I ran to my bathroom and looked in the mirror. Still bald. I looked pretty normal though.

I wouldn't say that I looked high. If there's a certain look for that.

There was a foul smell and I sniffed the air to find its source. I cupped my hand over my mouth and huffed out a puff of air. Good grief. When was the last time I brushed my teeth? I sniffed my underarms. Even bigger mistake. I hope I didn't reek like this when Darla was over.

I reached over to the shower and turned the knob to heat. After I threw my clothes on the floor I looked in the mirror and took a moment to look at myself. I was looking like an old man. It was never as though I was beefcake with muscles etched along my skin, but I'd surely never been this skinny.

Maybe Tony had been on to something.

As I hopped in the shower, I couldn't help but enjoy the steam and beads of water cascading down my skin. I reached for my toothbrush that was sitting on a shelf in the shower and brushed my teeth. After going a day without brushing them my teeth had begun growing fuzzy sweaters. It felt like heaven to rid them of the plaque. I finished lathering up and hopped out. Not having hair really deducts the time necessary to take a shower. I had been in a debate lately as to whether I should be using shampoo or body soap on my scalp. There's no hair right? But there are still follicles!

I grabbed the dangling towel and dried myself off. I couldn't help but notice the loose feeling of my sweatpants as I pulled them on.

"Crap," I said to myself when a thought passed me by. Tony had taken his goodies with him, right? I mean, he wouldn't be such an idiot to leave them sitting around the house….or would he?

I looked all over the bathroom and couldn't find them in there. I made my way searching through things around the house and couldn't find the baggie anywhere so I just assumed that he'd gathered his belongings before he left.

It was still amazing to me how much of an appetite I had when I smoked. It was somewhat relieving. Semi-enjoyable. Maybe I shouldn't really even say that I'd enjoy it seeing as how today was the first time I'd ever even smoked. If anything it was just tolerable. But for once I didn't feel like puking my brains out. And for once I felt like eating which might I say, I had missed the taste of food for a while.

One thing that wasn't too enjoyable was seeing Zippy. That was a white lie. I really did like seeing her, it's just everything that I begin to question when I'm around her that I don't like. She's my little hallucination. I would have thought that after having confronted the fact that I knew she wasn't real, it would've made me stop seeing her. I thought it would have been somewhat like laying the brick wall against my subconscious.

Maybe it was just the pot. I didn't think pot made you hallucinate but then again it could've just been my tumor. My tumor. Holy hell, a tumor. It makes me feel so old to say that. To be able to say 'I have ownership of a tumor'. I guess it's more of the tumor having ownership over me.

"My tumor," I said aloud, partially in hopes that it would make me come to the reality that, hey, I really do have one in my head. Or maybe I just said it aloud to make it less dramatic. But it is.

As far as Zippy goes, it's not that I necessarily don't enjoy her company. It's the simple fact that I know she's not real. That I know that this girl who I thought was so phenomenal, with this kickass personality and this gorgeous flowy long hair that I could only dream of getting lost in, is something that I made up on my own. That it wasn't even me making her up but the cancer pressing on exactly the right spot in my brain that had made her up. I must be one crappy person for it to not only take my own insanity to create a beautiful girl but a cancerous tumor to inflict a beautiful being on myself.

It freaks me out even more that my subconscious would create a character that believes she's an angel. I've never been one to believe in a higher being. Not to say that there isn't one. There's just never been a time that I really had the need to rely on a God. Although I never had my dad around, I had my mom to rely on. I guess I never really struggled with anything so extreme to the point of actually needing a God.

Which makes me wonder, if there are people out there my age who have such a declaration of their love for 'God', and they haven't gone through half the crap that me or my mom have gone through, why would they even need one?

Want to know what I think? I think that they're all full of crap and have no clue what's out there. They rely on something that was written about thousands of years ago. Something no more than really a book of fables and stories. Or that because they don't know what's out there that they'd rather have faith in something and find out it doesn't exist, than to have faith in nothing and find out that there is something and be screwed to a damnation in Hell which they could've easily avoided by believing in something.

Personally, even if at some point I had faith in a god, I really don't think that at this point in time I would still have that 'undying faith'. Why? Well, let's see here, cancer at fifteen. I think that's a pretty good reason why.

What the hell kind of cretin gives a fifteen year old cancer?

# Chapter 5

"JESUS CHRIST!" Shouted an angry mom.

"Did you see him!?" I yelled at my mom as I came running into the living room.

I came to a quick halt as I saw my mom standing in the middle of the living room angry as a beaver that's had to rebuild his damn dam ten times.

"Gabe, what is this?" My mom asked with her left hand on her hip and her right hand holding Tony's little baggie of natural remedies.

"Err, I swear it's not mine."

"Then pray tell, who does it belong to?"

I stared at her in long silence then looked around the room.

"There's no one here to look for, boy. Just me and you so if you're looking for someone to blame, that finger might as well be pointing at yourself."

"Tony and Darla came over this morning and made me breakfast."

"Well," she said, "then my guess is that this belongs to Tony."

"Why would you assume that? I mean Darla's pretty wild too."

"So it's hers?"

"I didn't say that."

"Then it's yours and they just came over and made breakfast for you and you randomly brought up the topic while I was questioning you about the weed just to divert my attention to something else?"

"No, it's Tony's."

"Why couldn't you just say that instead of playing games with my head?"

"Sorry."

"So," mom said as she headed off into the kitchen, "he and Darla came over to make you breakfast?"

"Yeah they were over here around eleven."

"Sounds more like lunch."

"I guess," I said as I followed her in. "It was nice being able to eat for once. Tasted pretty good too."

"I see. Should I assume Tony's little gift had something to do with your appetite."

"Yeah," I said ashamed that I had let my mom catch me the first time I ever tried weed. I mean, I'm sure parents catch their kids if they make a habit of it. But really? The first time? I've never been one to keep a secret well hidden.

"I don't want that stuff it in the house," she said as she searched the fridge, "But I also don't want you getting any skinnier."

"I'm not sure I understand what you're saying."

"I think you're a smart boy and if you used that noggin of yours a little bit you could figure out what I'm saying. I don't want Tony's little surprises sitting around in my house. I don't like the use of drugs in my home. Yet, at the same time I don't want my son feeling the way he does."

"Way to be vague."

"I like being vague, I also would like it if we're on a 'don't ask, don't tell' basis. There's nothing much to cook How's cereal sound?" She grabbed a couple boxes down from the cabinet. She shook a few boxes, all but one were empty. She stuck her hand in the box with cereal and took a few nibbles of some pieces. Her tongue fell out of her mouth and she scrapped the pieces off of her tongue, back into the box.

Turning towards me, she tossed the boxes in the trash and headed for the phone on the wall, "Better yet, how about we just order ourselves a pizza."

"Order Hawaiian. Salty and sweet and just all around deliciousness. Maybe with a cheese stuffed crust. Oh yeah, that sounds appetizing."

Mom eyeballed me for a few seconds and squinted her eyes. "Come here a second."

I walked over to her and she lifted my head to the light as she looked in my eyes. "What're you doing?"

"Well, you look sober. I'll order some a Hawaiian pizza." She picked up the phone as I walked over to the fridge to take a swig of milk.

"I'd smell that before drinking it out of the container," she said.

I took a big whiff and nearly fell out of my skin. A lump grew in my throat and my cheeks puffed up with air. "Oh, that's rancid. How long's that been in there?"

"No telling. I need to go grocery shopping soon."

"You're telling me."

Mom got off of the phone and had a seat at the kitchen table and waved me over. I found some orange juice in the fridge and poured both of us a glass and sat down with her.

"So, how are things going with you and Darla?"

"Good I guess."

"I'm just wondering. You haven't really had much to say about her and then all of the sudden she's over here cooking breakfast for you and Tony in the middle of the day, during a school day."

"I know. She was just being nice. Tony asked her to come over. He can't cook so he asked if she'd come over and help."

"Just being a good friend I guess."

"Yeah. That's it. I mean, Tony had to go to school but Darla left not too long after he did."

"Oh, so you and Darla were here at the house alone?" she asked as she swirled the juice in her cup and took a swig.

"Not long, really."

"I know that you and Darla are just friends but I want you to be able to make wise decisions when it comes to," she looked off, then back to me, "you know."

Oh jeeze. The talk. Somehow I had avoided having the talk with my mom my whole life.

"Mom, I barely have enough energy to raise my pinky finger. Do you really think that I could raise anything else?"

"When it comes to Darla? Yes."

"Holy crap mom, like she's just a friend. I mean we kissed but…"

"Y'all kissed? Here?"

"Where else would we have kissed? I haven't been to school in weeks."

"Gabe, I want you to be careful. She's a sweet girl but you guys are just fifteen years old."

"I have cancer mom. I think you can relax a little."

"Says the boy who left his dope sitting on the coffee table."

"Says the boy whose FRIEND left his dope sitting on the coffee table."

"I'm just being a mom and saying what I know is right." Then she turned and looked at me like she's never looked at me before. "I love you, Gabe. It's hard to know my little man is going through something that I can't control, that he shouldn't have to be dealing with at such a young age. So it's kind of nice to be able to just worry about normal mom things. About my boy doing drugs or having sex."

"I'm not having sex."

"Yet."

My mouth fell open.

"In the mood to catch flies?"

I shut my mouth and slumped back in my seat. "Not particularly, though I've heard they're full of protein."

"It's just nice to not have to worry about something so large scale for once. Something I can bug you about," and she leaned across the table towards me and kissed me on the head.

The doorbell rang.

"Time for some Hawaiian style pizza," she said as her eyebrows danced.

●

The next afternoon I decided I'd get out of the house and walk over to my spot. My little overlook. The same overlook that my dad died at. The same old overlook that I met Zippy at. The same overlook that I sat at when I found out that I had cancer.

As I walked down the hill I realized that it wasn't going to be Zippy that I met there this time, but Tony.

"Well, well, well. If it isn't my man Gabe," said Tony as I sat down beside him.

"What's up? I didn't think I'd find you here."

"Yeah I'm not really usually one to sit and admire nature. I'd rather be admiring the girls walking around in nature."

"This I know. So what's up? Dad mad at you skipping class? Kick you out of the house?"

"Nah, I'm just hanging out."

"It would've been funnier if he kicked you out."

"Cancer's making you feisty, aint it?"

"Nah just making me take things in as they are."

"I know what you mean. I've just been sitting out here the past few hours, thinking. You know. Trying to see what it is that you see when you sit here."

"Oh jeez not you too," for a split second I felt more like a freak than a friend.

"Not me too what?"

"You're freaking out on me."

"Hah, dude I'm not freaking out on you. I'm just thinking, you know how young we are and well, you're my best friend. It's been that way for as long as I can remember and I just don't know what I'd do without my partner in crime."

"I'm not going anywhere so you can give up this game. Let it go. Let that idea die homie." After a minute of silence I continued, "Jeez, I'm here now. Quit being a baby on me. If anyone should be being acting like a wimp it's me."

"What're you talking about? You already are a wimp." Tony said nudging me. "So what happened after I left?"

"What do you mean? I basically slept all day."

"Not so easy." He looked at me, nodded and licked his lips, "I mean with Darla. When I left yesterday Darla was still at your house. We have seventh period together and she wasn't there. Did you, you know?"

"I'm not sure what you're talking about. She left my house about thirty minutes after you did."

"That's weird. But thirty minutes is beyond enough time to, uh, 'brown chicken, brown cow'," he said in a sing song voice.

"We kissed. That's it."

"Right and that's why she wasn't able to get to school at all yesterday?"

"No seriously. Right after you left, we kissed. I fell on the ground and she helped me up and left."

He started laughing, "Woah, hang on a second. You fell after you kissed her?"

"I was sitting on the counter beside her and fell. So what?"

"All I'm saying is no wonder she left."

"But she didn't go to school?"

"Nah, she wasn't there today either. I just assumed she went back for seconds at your place."

"No, yesterday she left my house at like 1:30, seventh period starts at what? Like 2:15? That should've been more than enough time for her to get back to class."

"You didn't call her last night? I mean after her kissing you and all?"

"No, you were so smart that you left your little baggie sitting on my mom's coffee table and I didn't even think about Darla before going to bed."

"Jeez dude, I thought I'd leave it for you. I knew you wouldn't accept it if I offered but I surely thought you would've been smart enough to have stashed it." He took a pause. "And please, I doubt that you didn't even think about Darla before going to bed last night. She's been walking through your dreams since she gave you that extra lollipop in fourth grade."

"How did you know about the lollipop?"

"Everyone knows about the lollipop. You might wanna head over to Darla's house though. Probably let her down without calling her. Made her little heart break so bad she couldn't show her face around school."

"She said she'd call me."

"That's a good one. You're the guy. How about this," he said as he poked me with his finger, "Go ahead and let your balls drop and crawl over to Darla's house and see what's up."

"Fine," I said as I stood up. "I know when I'm no longer wanted."

As Tony put it, I let my balls drop and headed over to Darla's house. Of course, to see 'what's up'. As I walked up the ridiculous driveway that led to Darla's house I couldn't help but think about the fact that other than the party where Jake beat me up, I hadn't been there since her 10<sup>th</sup> birthday party. It was really the last birthday party that any kid had that was still a co-ed party. Ten years old and under you can be friends with girls or boys but when you hit eleven and start needing deodorant you only like the other gender as a play thing. Be it for your heart or body. Puberty, the divider of the sexes.

I walked up the brick doorsteps and rang the doorbell. Darla's mom answered it. I was nearly thrown off guard at the striking resemblance of the mother and daughter. She had the same green eyes and straight brown hair. Even her stature and height were on point. Looking at her mom was like looking at Darla twenty years in the future.

"Oh, Gabe. Now's not really the best time sweetie." She looked at me pitying. I wasn't sure if she meant now's not the best time because I have cancer and they don't want their daughter dating a boy who could drop dead at any moment, or if it wasn't a good time because they were doing something.

"Oh. I'm sorry Mrs. Lively, should I come back later? I just wanted to talk to Darla. I had seen Darla yesterday," I tried my best not to give away the fact that Darla had been over to my house while she should've been at school. Sometimes the front office would call if you skipped a class but sometimes it got glitch and would skip houses. I could only hope, for the fact that I'd look like a decent person that her parents didn't know that she'd ditched school to hang out with me. "It was just in passing really, but I wanted to apologize for not calling her yesterday."

"I'll relay the message to her. It's good to see you," she said as she began to shut the door.

"You know," I said as I dug for something to keep her at the door. She must've found out that Darla had skipped school to be with me. Why else wouldn't she want me to see her? I still couldn't be too sure. "I'm not sure if you know my friend Tony. He's about my height, Latino?"

"Sounds familiar, why?"

"Well, Tony and I were talking a little while ago and he mentioned that he didn't see Darla in class yesterday or today and while he doesn't have the best attendance, I know she does. I just wanted to check in on her." Then I forced a smile, trying to smile reassuringly but it just turned out to be, what I'm sure was creepy, with one side corner of my mouth lifted, and the other falling flat.

She let out a big sigh, "Come in, Gabe."

"Oh, ok." I walked inside the house and her mom led me through to their den.

"I should probably tell you that Darla had a little bit of an accident on the way back to class from your house yesterday."

I stopped in my tracks. All hopes of her mom being clueless about Darla skipping had washed away. Crap. On top of her knowing that Darla skipped, she knows it was so that she could be over at my house.

"I'm sorry she skipped, ma'am. She and my friend Tony were just trying to cheer me up is all."

She turned back towards and stared, as if to tell me something without having to move her lips. It hit me.

"You said she had an accident?"

"Yes, I did."

"What kind of an accident?"

"Less of an accident. More of a Jake."

"I'm not sure if I follow what you're saying." Then I looked at her and realized that something bad had happened.

"Gabe, Jake hurt Darla."

Tears welled up in my eyes, I looked like a wimp. Scared, I just stared at her. Speechless.

"Come. Have a seat."

Mrs. Lively brought me into the den to sit with her. She poured me a glass of lemonade and handed it to me. I took a swig and it was definitely homemade, I could tell because of the tingling acidity.

"She was on her way back to school," her mom began, "from your house. Jake was outside walking to his weight training class in the weight room out near the corner of campus. Darla was running up out of the woods and he saw her running in his peripheral vision. When he saw her running up to scool, he dashed over to her. He began asking her where she was coming from and when she told him he became irate. Rather than using his anger to fuel what could've been an intense work out, he took it out on Darla."

"Is she okay?" I asked, feeling the size of a mouse.

"She's a little roughed up but she'll be fine." She hesitated a minute, then offered, "Would you like to see her? It would make her day a little brighter, I'm sure."

"Of course, she's here?"

"Yes, she's upstairs."

I couldn't help but be worried. Darla was really the only girl to ever make me feel as though I wasn't that much of a loser. Mrs. Lively led me down the hall, around the banister, and up to her room.

Standing outside of her bedroom, Mrs. Lively said, "Now, don't be too surprised. She got pretty roughed up."

I nodded.

"Knock, knock." Mrs. Lively chanted.

"I'm fine mom. Just reading, I promise," said Darla in a tender voice. It's amazing that even though this girl had been beaten up by an evil monster that she still would be so sweet.

"You have a visitor honey."

Darla lifted her gaze up from her book and saw it was me. For a split second her face lit up as bright as the morning sun, then she paled over and crawled her head beneath her frilly pillow.

"Oh, Gabe! I look horrible."

"No, you don't," I said as I walked towards the window seat.

"I'll leave you two alone," said Mrs. Lively as she left the doorway and closed the door behind her.

I sat on the window seat for a few seconds before she peeked an eye out from beneath the pillow. She sighed and uncovered her face. There were bruises scattered all over her. Her left eye was a greenish purple hue and her mouth was ten times the size it usually was. Even her cheeks were swollen. She looked somewhat reminiscent of a chipmunk that'd gotten into a fight with an alley cat.

"He really did a number on you, didn't he?"

"Yeah," she nodded and sat up.

"Darla, despite that jerk bruising you up, you still look beautiful, with or without makeup." I stared at her trying my best to keep the tears from cascading down my face. Anger started to burn inside of me at the thought of Jake doing this to Darla. "Why did he do this?"

"I guess he was jealous."

"So what? He's jealous of you spending time with some guy who has cancer so he beats up the girl he dated for four years? That's horrible. I spent the past six years tripping over your every word and was overly jealous of any guy who had the opportunity to spend five seconds of you, yet I'd never hurt you."

"I know," she said as she studied me, "you're really a great guy. You know that right?"

"If I'm so great then why does it take six whole years to make the girl of my dreams realize that?"

"Maybe she just didn't want to risk it? Or maybe she liked you so much that she was too scared to be anything more than a friend?"

"Maybe if that girl wouldn't have been so scared of messing up a friendship, she wouldn't have ended up having her ass thrown to her by some jerk."

Her jaw nearly fell open. It probably would have if her cheeks weren't so swollen.

"I'm sorry. I'm just annoyed. Not with you, but with Jake."

"No, you're right. If I had just chosen the right guy from the start none of this would've happened."

"It's not your fault this happened. You're a great girl and a great friend. No matter what, you'll always be my friend."

"Maybe I'd like to be more than 'just friends'.

"Sure it's not because you feel pity on me for being a baldy?"

"Nah, it's because you have cancer."

"Wow."

"Just kidding," she said with a smirk.

"So," I said getting up from the window seat and sitting down next to her on her bed, "where is

Jake anyways? I'd like to have talk with that little turd."

"The last time y'all talked it didn't go over very well did it?"

"No. But last time he was out to hurt me. This time he hurt you."

"Don't waste your time worrying about it."

"Why not?" I asked.

"I'm not planning on tagging around with him if that's what you're thinking."

"You'd make good money as a psychic."

"Jake's parent's shipped him out."

"He just beat you up yesterday, though? How could his parents have gotten a hold of him so quick?"

"Turns out that was the last straw that his parents needed. With his dad's office time running out next year he didn't want a bad name in the public eye."

"That makes sense. I've got a bad taste for them myself, because of the fact that they were able to spawn such an insane creature."

"Yeah, no kidding. Yesterday, I ran straight home after he got a hold of me. My mom was home and I just threw myself on her and starting bawling. She got on the phone with Jake's parents, while we were on our way to the hospital."

"It's a good thing."

"Definitely and apparently when Jake had gotten a hold of you it made his parents realize that maybe, just maybe, their son wasn't the little angel they always thought he'd been."

"Well then I'm glad he beat me up. At least then it gave them some reason to think he could've beat you up too."

"Yeah I guess I'm glad he did too, when you put it that way."

"I really don't think his parents were too convinced that he was such a bad kid. They kept throwing out, 'well maybe he was provoked', after he beat you up. I think that thought escaped them when they heard he'd beat me up too."

"I would hope they wouldn't be stupid enough to think you'd provoke him."

"Of course they wouldn't. They're pretty ignorant when it comes to their son but they're not blind."

"Yeah, so where'd he go?" I was itching to find out. I hoped she wasn't going to say a few towns over. Jake's crazy ass would end up finding his way to my house in the middle of the night. My luck I'd wake up in the middle of the night to some large shadow hovering over my bed.

"Oh, right. So after my mom called and told his folks everything that happened they called one of his relatives up in Missouri. They sent him out on a red-eye last night. By the time he got home they'd already bought the tickets and packed his bags for him."

"I wish I would've seen his face. Would've made my day. Better yet my year."

"Mine too. I'm glad. Without him around…"

"There's less of a chance of me getting beat up for sneaking glimpses of you."

She let out a huge laugh and sigh of relief. "Yeah. Exactly."

That's when she leaned in and stared in my eyes. Those big green eyes. I swear, between her dark brown hair and her sultry green eyes, she has me like putty in her hands. Then she took me by surprise and grabbed the nape of my neck. We kissed. A long, hard, amazing kiss. Her lips and tongue tasted of peppermint. Somehow, with no makeup on, messy hair, and bruises all over her body and face, she still managed to have that amazing smell of cocoa butter.

I had been staring at her for at least five minutes before I even realized that I was staring.

"Sorry about being such a freak."

"It's ok. You've always been a bit of a freak. I knew that from the get go."

"What?"

"It's ok, honestly."

"You really are beautiful, you know that?"

"Holy crap. Did you have a little visit from Tony before you came over here? I mean I look like I was hit by a train."

"No, you just are captivating. And in theory, given how big of a guy Jake is and all, you basically were hit by a train."

"You're so funny, Gabe. Real funny." She swallowed hard, "Thank God he's gone."

The door creaked open and Darla's dad stuck his head in and I jumped up from where I was sitting on her bed.

"Hey guys, I brought some food up. Not too sure if you're hungry or not, Gabe, but I thought I'd bring you some too. That wife of mine makes a mean beef stew. I figured that even if you weren't hungry, just the smell of it would make you salivate."

"Thanks, Mr. Lively," I said.

Mr. Lively looked at me then at Darla a couple times and chuckled. "It's good to see you, Gabe."

"Good to see you too sir." I looked over to a mirror above one of Darla's dressers and I was as red as a tomato.

Darla's dad left the room for us to talk over stew. I didn't have the heart not to eat it after her dad brought it up. So I ate and ate. I also managed to keep my food down the whole time I was visiting her.

Once I was on the way home, that was another story. I puked my brains out on the side of the road. And it was some really good food but nothing tastes as good coming up as it did going down.

●

Mom had to work the evening shift at the restaurant tonight. Fine by me. Darla's parents had already made me a home cooked meal.

Would you look at that? The girl of my dreams had me over for dinner to meet the folks. Not exactly how I'd planned it or the way I would've wanted to sit down to meet them as her boyfriend. Given the fact that we'd been in school together since kindergarten her parents already knew me so it wasn't even really a matter of meeting them. It was just that sense of being there for her and her parents knew that I was the guy she liked. Or the reason she got her arse kicked.

I traveled to my spot. My little overlook. The lights twinkled across the valley as dusk set in.

"I've missed you my little friend." Once again the sing-song voice of angels. Or angel. Singular. I looked around. Yes, singular. As far as I could see at least.

"Well I hate to say it Zippy but I haven't really had time to think about missing you."

"Yowza, you're still pretty bruised about me coming out of the heaven closet, aren't you?"

"I guess. You must've fallen pretty hard to end up where you are."

"What do you mean?"

"Oh, you know. Being an angel of death and all."

Zippy took a few steps back and put her hand on her chest, offended. "I am not an angel of death."

"Alright then, whateveeever you say. Anyway, I've been too busy to really give much thought to you."

"I know. You've been busy with Darla. Jake really got a hold of her, eh?"

"Yeah, it's OK though, his parents sent him off to Missouri. It turns out that they didn't want their little prize football star's bad turn of events to rain on the campaign parade."

"Well, it's good that he's off to Missouri but maybe it's a blessing in disguise to have had someone pick on you a little. A shame that he took his feelings out on you and Darla but there is a little bit of a silver lining."

"Oh yeah, Darla gets to be a lovely new shade of polka dot."

"I didn't mean that. I just was thinking that, I mean you don't see the bright side to what all has happened?"

"Not sure that I'm catching your drift. In fact you're kind of ticking me off."

"Gabe, I'm not trying to make you angry. I'm just saying to look on the bright side. You would've never known about your cancer had you not gotten attacked by him. And now you have a chance to restore things to the way they should've been."

"Oh, yeah Zippy. It's great to have restored my friendship with Darla because we both got beat up by the ogre."

"Not exactly what I meant but maybe you would've never had the guts to befriend Darla again after the incident with Jake if you didn't feel like you had a reason to take chances. Maybe you're really only up for taking chances now that you have less to lose."

"Less to lose?"

"And who knows maybe it was a blessing in disguise that Darla got hurt simply because of the fact that it made Jake's own parents realize how much of a monster he was. Sadly sometimes it takes a bad situation to make people realize how much of a change is needed in their life."

"Ah, so this is about to be one of those situations where you tell me I need to start changing up my life, huh?"

"Well that's not exactly what I was trying to hint around at. But maybe instead of sulking around you should try and make use of yourself."

"Look angel girl, I'm fine. My life is fine. I've got cancer yes. But you, you're getting to be a pain in my rear."

She finally sat down next to me instead of standing over me, "I'm just trying to offer a word of the wise to someone who may need to open his heart up a little to God."

"Zippy! Don't you get it? Why would I open myself up like that? I've never had a strong connection to a God. Just so you know my life, be it that I have cancer, is really okay."

"And you're fine with just getting by with an 'okay' life? Why not spend your life to the fullest? No one knows who's here today and tomorrow."

"I'm fine with the life I have now Zip. Cool it. So what if I'm here today and gone tomorrow?

Everyone at some point or another is here today and gone tomorrow, isn't that what you were telling me the other day? The whole reason why I shouldn't have been drowning myself in self-pity? Now you're going back on what you said I should be doing?"

"There's a difference in self-pity and self-awareness."

I held my hand up to her, "I'll see you around. Better yet, how about you just leave me alone for a little while. I'm tired of having my parade rained on by an angel. Go show someone else how perfect you are. I'm good."

I walked away from her.

"Gabe, you can't walk away from me forever."

I turned back and shot her a look of disgust. "Oh yes I can!"

"You can run but you can't hide."

"Leave me alone!" I shouted as I walked on.

"I'll see you in a few days."

"I'll walk away from you then too." I waited for her to shout something back at me but she didn't. Finally, when I'd reached the top of the hill I turned around and she was gone.

I wish I had the capability to disappear like she did.

As far as I'm concerned I'm fine in what I believe in or the lack thereof. I don't know if I believe in a higher being or not but I'm not going to go mindlessly falling into the arms of some God

141

who I never had faith in and am only turning to in a tough point in my life. I'm better than that. And wouldn't that just be admitting to myself that I'm giving up? That I have no control, so I should hope aimlessly that there's someone else out there who can control things for me?

●

Both of my parents were Christians. Notice that I said 'were', not 'are'. My dad's dead so anything that he was is now in past tense. As far as my mom goes, I'm not really sure as to whether or not my mom still has faith. Given that we hadn't gone to church since I was a little boy I really don't know.

Ready for a little time travel? Alright. Let's go.

Picture this: little boy, three foot tall. Brown shaggy hair and big brown eyes to match. Can you guess who it is? ME!

Anyways, it had been about two weeks since my dad died. The first week after he died we didn't go to church. My mom had her head wrapped around the funeral and had bigger things to deal with than making her face seen at church. The following week my mom insisted on going. She felt that even though my dad wasn't there to go with us we still were alive and kicking and had enough of a reason to go to church and be thankful for what we still had.

It was a little white church that sat on a hill. Inside the church there was a small greeting area with a church office to the right and a staircase leading downstairs to the Sunday school area. Just past the greeting area were the doors to the sanctuary. Inside the little room were ten rows of pews lining opposite sides of the room. It smelled like old people and feet.

We took our usual seat midway through the room.

"I'm so sorry for your loss, Sheila," said a grey haired woman in her 80's.

"Luke was a wonderful man," the preacher's wife told her before the sermon. She was in her early 50's and her eyebrows had been waxed and drawn on in a way that made her look like she was always a mixture of angry, sad, and surprised. She wore blue eye shadow that she painted all the way up to her eyebrows and donned a bright red lipstick. Her hair was a platinum blonde and the tight permed hair stood at least five inches off of her head. Although she looked like a drag queen from the neck up, from the shoulders down she was always fairly plain. Her outfits rarely strayed from the neutral tones of brown, beige, and tan.

The youth pastor's wife came and sat down with us. Since her children and husband were always taking part in the Sunday school lesson, she always sat with us.

"You know, Sheila, if you ever need anything Max and I would love to help out. Even if you guys need a place to get away to here and there, we have an extra guest room."

"Thank you, if we do need anything you'll be the first person I call."

The sermon began and we sat and listened. Usually I would be in the nursery with my friends but that week my mom kept me with her.

At the end of the sermon the wide and balding preacher began to speak to the congregation about my dad dying.

"Before we pray I wanted to talk a little about a young fellow I knew pretty well and considered a son at a distance. This young man's name was Luke Perkins and he was one of the best examples of a Christian as I ever had seen in my day. I remember the day his parents had him and I remember him as a young adolescent. He was a rambunctious little tike, a true boy at heart playing in the dirt. Freaking little girls out by putting bugs in their hair. I remember one day going over to his parents' house for Sunday dinner. As I was walking up the gravel driveway to the doorstep I was hit with this painful pinging in my right leg. I looked down at it and I had been hit by a B. B." The congregation began laughing, "You think it's funny and in hindsight it might've been but that B.B. was painful. The strangest part about it was there was no one around! I looked all around and then my eyes spotted this little freckle faced boy peeking out from behind a bush. Sure, I could've been mad but when I walked around the bush and found him cowering there, I asked him, 'Did you hit me with this B.B.?' And to my surprise he said, 'Yes, sir. I did.' I scruffed his hair up a little bit and told him not to worry and to just come on inside with me for dinner. He was a good little boy. I don't remember him ever telling a lie. Sure, he'd get into some trouble here or there but you always knew you could trust your word with that one."

The pastor took a handkerchief out of his pocket to wipe the tears falling down from his eyes. "I knew that boy was going to really make something of himself. He did. He would go out of his way to help anyone in need. I remember on a missionary trip to Mexico he literally gave a stranger walking down the road the shirt off of his back. I didn't have the heart to tell him the man was probably so hot that he didn't need to have a shirt on."   Once again the congregation laughed. It was a bittersweet laughter as they lingered in the happy memories.

The pastor continued, "That young man grew up and married a beautiful young woman and had a son. Unfortunately, as many of you already know, Luke passed away this weekend at the hand of a careless drunk driver on the way home from working the graveyard shift. I wish there was a way for us to give back at least half of what Luke gave to the world to his family. Although money cannot fill the wounds that this young mother and son are feeling, we surely need to do the best we can to help them out in this time of need. Let us pray and then collect up an offering for the family."

The praying began.

It was great for my mom to have the financial support from the church. Though the money from the church didn't cover everything it covered more than his life insurance, which was practically non-existent. Fortunately for us we had the church to help us out.

After the sermon we left the church and headed back to our car. When we got to the car my mom buckled me into my car seat and turned around to see the youth pastor walking up to our car.

"Hi Sheila," he said as he walked up to her at the car. "I'm so sorry about what happened to Luke. You know he and I were pretty close growing up."

"I know, Max. It's alright. We got God looking out for us. I mean, it's not alright, but everything happens for a reason, right?" She asked him as she tried to forget that they were talking about her husband being dead. He was her high school sweetheart.

"Yeah, you're right. It does. You know, me and the Mrs.' would love to make dinner for you and Gabe one night. I'm sure y'all are having a tough time. We'd love to be of some help."

"That sounds lovely. We'd enjoy that."

"Well, I'll have a little chat with my wife and give you a ring."

"I'll be listening out for it."

Later that evening my mom had given me a bath and had settled into her own p.j.s when the doorbell rang. It wasn't too late, maybe around six and she was about to get started on dinner. She went to the door to see who it was. When she peeked through the little window on the door she realized it was just Max. He had a big box with him. After realizing it was just him, my mom opened the door.

"Well what a welcome surprise!"

"I brought some food over that Sarah made, looks like a few casserole dishes and a pie. Given the size I'd say it should last you a week."

"That's so generous of you guys," my mom looked out the door towards his car. "Sarah didn't come with you?"

"No, she stayed at home to get the kids ready for school."

"Oh, alright," my mom reached for the box.

"I'll bring this in for you. It's pretty heavy."

"Yeah, of course," she let him in. "If you want you can just sit the box on the counter and I'll put the food in the fridge."

"Alright," he put the box on the counter and brushed his hands against each other.

"Thank you for everything, Max. I didn't expect for you to bring anything over for us tonight," she said with a big smile on her face. "It's a pleasant surprise."

"No problem, Sheila. I went home and me and Sarah got to talking about making some food for you guys. Figured there was no time better than today to get started making y'all some dinner." He looked at the dishes, "Honestly it may last you longer than a week if you freeze it. Don't worry about bringing the dishes back over. We've got plenty."

"Thank you so much, tell your wife I said thank you, won't you?"

"I sure will," He started to head to the door and he stopped in his own footsteps. "You know, there is something that I wanted to talk to you about." He looked over toward me, and then continued, "You think we could talk in private?"

Confused she responded, "I guess I can put him in his room for a minute."

She put me in my room but when she left I ran over to the door and cracked it open to watch and listen. I was nosey that way. She came back and sat on the couch by the youth pastor.

"What is it that you needed to talk to me about? Something about Luke? Anything I should know?"

"Well," he said as he brushed his pant legs off. He looked at her and pursed his lips. "There is actually something, but I think I should show you, instead of tell you."

"Oh," my mom said as she scratched her head, "I'm a little confused?"

He leaned in towards her and tried to kiss her, but she shoved him away.

"MAX! What are you doing?"

"Come on, Sheila. You know you've felt the same feelings for me as I have for you all these years. The waving at church," he waited for her to say something, but when she didn't he continued. "Come on, me offering to make you and Gabe dinner."

"You make me and Gabe dinner? Your wife made us dinner, you just brought it over?"

"But who offered it? Me. You didn't know that was me coming on to you?"

"Max, it was a nice gesture. It's something that many people at the church do to help people who are going through a rough patch."

He leaned back and stared at my mom like she was crazy, "You know what I was talking about. You're just too scared now that you have the chance to act on it."

"I think you're a little bit confused. I mean," my mom tried to push back the tears. "My husband just died barely two weeks ago." When he didn't say anything, she continued, "I think you ought to leave."

"Oh yeah right! After I take time out of my day to bring you and your rug rat food for the whole week, you expect me to just leave?"

"Well I don't know what you think you're going to get in return, mister, but you're not getting anything like that from me."

"Is that so?" He leaned in and stared my mom down for a good five seconds before throwing her on the couch and forcing himself on her.

Mom started screaming. I got mad that someone was hurting my mommy and ran out and shouted, "Leave my mommy alone!"

"Gabe, go get the neighbors!"

"I'll be damned if he does," shouted Max, "you better tell that boy of yours to get his little ass back into his room." Then he pulled a gun out of his back pocket and pointed it at my mom's head. "Go ahead, tell him."

My mom's eyes widened, "Gabe," she forced a smile, "Sweetie. It's ok. Just go to your room."

"Mommy?"

"Yes honey," she nodded. "It's ok."

I watched that corrupt man put the gun against my mom's head as he waited for me to go back into my room. I curled up into a ball inside of my closet and cried myself to sleep.

That was the last time we ever went to church. My mom hasn't ever really talked about there being a God after that happened. But could you really blame her?

# Chapter 6

"Look-a-there," said mom resting her hand on my face as she sat on the corner of my bed. "If that isn't the most handsome boy I ever have met."

"You always were a sucker for baldies," I joked back.

"Ever since you were born," she looked at me as though she wanted to say something but was holding back.

"What's that face for?"

"Nothing," then she started spilling the beans. The beans, of course, that I already knew about. "I talked to Jake's parents today about some of the costs for the chemo."

"Yeah?"

"Turns out that he had a run in with Darla after she was over here the other day."

"I know, mom."

"Oh. Then I'm guessing you also know that they sent him away."

"Yeah."

"Honey, you realize that they sent him away because of the campaign coming up in the next year, right?"

"No, they sent him away because he beat up two kids from his high school. One of which was his ex-girlfriend, who he'd just recently broken up with. He's a woman beater."

"Gabe, I'm not sure it was as much the fact that he beat you and Darla up that he was sent away as you think it was."

"Well it's the main part."

"But in addition to that it's probably mostly because his dad has a campaign coming up next year."

"Ok?"

"Alright, let me start over," She looked at me and contemplated before continuing. She could tell that I was completely and utterly lost. "So, you understand that they sent him away to not drag their name through mud anymore, right?

"Of course. Who would want their kid, who by the way is a monster, running around town ruining their family name?"

"No one I would assume." She paused and continued realizing that what she was trying to relay wasn't catching on, "However they do have a campaign coming up next year."

"Yes! You've said this a million times now."

"Well that's only because you're not catching on. The Jenkins' campaign is next year. That means that they're probably going to have to fork out a good bit of money towards the running of that campaign."

"Are you trying to tell me that they aren't going to be able to help with chemo just because of the campaign they're doing next year? I mean I may not even be alive by next year. What does it matter if they pay a few more months on it?"

"Gabe, calm down. And don't say things like that. It breaks my heart." She pulled the pony tail holder out and let her hair blonde hair fall onto her shoulders. "They still want to be able to help, but they aren't going to be able to help in the way that they have been helping. Now that they shipped Jake off to Missouri they're going to be paying for his private school out there as well as money for his family to let him stay with him. All that on top of a campaign. It just means we may have to do some fundraising."

"But who would even come to a fundraiser for me? If you haven't noticed I'm not the most popular guy in town. In fact, I got beat up by the one who was."

"Well, I talked to Darla's parents today." She said, her face coming back to life again."

"Oh yeah?"

"Yeah. I mean, you remember when Darla talked to me at the hospital when you were getting your biopsy done?"

"Of course."

"Well even then they were planning on helping out, you knew that. When we talked today they said that they'd help sponsor a carnival fundraiser for you. It would be primarily sponsored by their store but anyone in town wanting to help out would be able to also."

"But I was just over there this afternoon with Darla. They didn't mention anything to me about it."

"Maybe they wanted it to come from me. You're OK with this right?"

"Oh feeling like more of a freak than I already do. Sure, why not? It's just in front of the whole town."

"It's a good thing, sweetie."

"Yeah I guess so." A thought pinged in my head, "Hey, they could have a freak tent. You know the kind with bearded ladies and insanely strong men. And then they can just throw me in there too because well hell I'm just as freakish as they are, right?"

"This crap you're doing right here is working my nerves. Someone tries to do something nice for you and you totally turn everything into a bad thing. It's good. Stop with this. Alright?"

"Yeah, sure."

I gave my mom a hug and she stood up to go to her room.

"I love you."

"I love you too."

"Better."

She walked down the hall and turned the lights out in the house.

At six that morning I heard tapping at my window.

Once.

Twice.

I draped the covers over my head and grunted. I did everything I could do to ignore the constant tapping.

Caplink.

Caplink.

Finally I crawled out of bed, dragging the covers with me. I looked out and saw it was Tony. Tony my homie. Waking me up at six in the morning when he knows good and well that I'm for no visitors at this time of night. Er, morning.

I cracked the window open and gazed at him. I wasn't even gazing at him, but through him.

"Hey sleepy head," he said.

"What're you doing here?"

"That's a wonderful way to greet your best friend."

"My best friend would know that I'm exhausted and that I just want to sleep."

"Your best friend may know that anyways and just not care. Besides there's a chance that your friend may have brought you something to take your aches and pains away," he said referencing his book bag.

"My mom's asleep down the hall. She doesn't want it in the house and I'm not so sure that I do either. I have chemo this afternoon."

"All the more reason for me to be here."

"What if she smells it?"

"She's asleep isn't she?"

"Yeah?"

"Well....." he said nudging to his book bag.

"If I get caught again you're going to have hell to pay." I opened the window up all the way and looked out, "Grab the lawn chair over there and climb in."

He climbed in the window and crashed on the floor.

"Jeeze, are you serious?"

"What?"

I walked over to my bedroom door and looked into the hallway just to be sure my mom hadn't woken up.

"You're nuts. You better be doing well in school, you'd make a horrible robber."

"You're hungry. That's hunger anger. Gabe, you're just 'hangry'." He took his bag off of his shoulders and grabbed his bag of illegal goodies and tossed them to me, "SMOKE. I'm tired of dealing with a hangry Gabe."

So we did because nobody likes to be around an angry Gabe. Especially not a hungry, angry, hangry Gabe. Even though I can't stand the idea of food.

"What time do you have chemo?" Tony asked.

"I dunno. Why? You think this stuff will mess chemo up? Like make it so that it doesn't take?"

"I don't think so. That would be weird."

"Why ask?"

"I was just thinking, you know. Maybe I could go with you."

"What? Why would you want to go with me?"

"Company? I mean crap I don't know, never mind it was a bad idea."

"It's not that it's a bad idea. It just takes forever. With your attention span you'd be like wandering the halls looking for candy bars and stuff. Or like, flirting with nurses."

"It was only two hours last week though, right?"

"Yeah but that was a Bleo only day. Today I have an EP infusion. Those take all day. Like six or seven hours."

"Yeah, I have no clue what you're talking about. You're right I'd probably go nuts."

"Welcome to my life."

I drifted off to sleep.

An hour later I was woken by the stomping of feet walking down the hall. I looked over at Tony and whispered in a loud angry whisper, "TONY! Dude, my mom's awake! What do we do?"

"We? That's your mom. Not mine," Tony said as he started putting his headphones back in his book bag to make his clean get away.

"What happened to you being my best friend at six am?"

"Well the same guy that was your best friend at six am happens to be the same guy who's scared crapless of angry moms."

Tony stood up and put his book bag on his shoulders. He began opening the window just when my mom slung the door wide open.

"Well, well, well. Looks like I caught a couple of potheads red handed," mom said with her hands on her hips.

"Ms. Perkins, I'm not too sure what you're talking about."

"Oh and what is it exactly that you're doing standing near the window with your bag on? About to make your getaway?"

"No ma'am," he said with a smile, "I'm just opening the window for a little fresh air."

"Tony, don't play dumb with me. Can you even see out of your eyes right now?"

"What's she talking about?" he asked me. His eyes were so narrow, I could barely even tell if they were open. Had Tony always been Asian?

"Maybe if you weren't so stoned," my mom said as she walked into the middle of the room and picked up a plastic baggie, "you would've realized you haven't even put your little goody bag into your book bag."

Tony looked at his stash in my mom's hands and his mouth fell open. He had packed up his textbooks and MP3 player, but of course he'd forgotten to stash his stash.

"And don't even try to play it off as being oregano. I'm young, but I wasn't born yesterday," continued mom as she stood staring us down.

"I'm sorry Ms. Perkins," Tony said, about to make an attempt to cover his hide, "I was just thinking, you know, I mean I don't really ever smoke this stuff. I was just thinking that it could be a pretty good idea to help Gabe feel better." He looked over at me then back at my mom, "I have to admit that I may be on to something. I mean doesn't he look better to you?"

My mom rolled her eyes, "He looks stoned out of his mind to me. Gabe, get up off the damn floor. You two follow me to the bathroom."

"Jesus Christ," Tony said under his breath, as we both stood up and followed my mom like two little ducklings about to be put in a row.

"You should've been thinking about Jesus before you brought that weed into my house," she said without turning around.

We followed her into the hall bathroom and watched as she emptied the contents of the Ziploc bag into the toilet.

"And this is your brain on drugs," she said as she flushed the toilet. "She turned toward us and sighed, "Sit," she said pointing towards the edge of the bath tub. We shrugged at each other and took a seat.

"Now you two listen up for a minute. I'm sure that may seem a bit difficult at the moment but try if you will."

She looked at us. I looked at Tony and he looked at me, for approval. We shrugged and nodded in agreement and sat down.

"Tony, I told Gabe not to bring this stuff into my home. I know good and well that my son isn't feeling up to his normal self. I also know good and well that if this stuff is found in my home it'll be hell to pay for the likes of you." She turned her focus towards the mirror and began putting makeup on, "However, another thing I know is that you've been helping him feel better but let's not do it here. Do you two understand me?" She looked back at the two of us.

"Yes ma'am," Tony and I said in unison.

"Alright then," said mom. "Gabe you have chemo this afternoon. Go rest up. As for you Tony, I'm pretty sure your dad would be hell-bent if he found out that you were skipping school again. So how about you not skip school again for a while and I'll forget the fact that you brought illegal drugs into my house." She finished dabbing a little mascara and lipstick on and escorted us back to my room.

"Well this all sounds good to me, Sheila," Tony said, his balls apparently larger when stoned.

"Boy you have got to be the boldest kid I've ever met. Go on to school. Gabe, go watch TV or something and try and rest up!"

My mom watched as Tony hopped out the window, under her breath she mumbled, "The nerve of that kid."

●

I tried my best to rest up but after about an hour I realized that the rest I was hoping for just wasn't going to come.

My mom was going to make breakfast, but she realized she was out of eggs, along with everything else so she went into town to pick some groceries up. Even though she said she'd be back soon, I knew she was going to be gone for a while.

There was no other perfect time to get out of the house, than now. Although I loved heading over to the overlook, Zippy was usually not too far behind me. I needed peace. Somewhere I could be alone where I knew she wouldn't ever be able to find me.

I walked out the back door and went over to the back of the chain link fence that surrounded our little house. I opened the gate and began heading down the same trail I had walked a million times as a little boy. It was a secluded trail shaded by large lush trees that were so wide you knew they were a few hundred years old. There were bushes with berries along the path. Growing up I'd grab some of the berries and eat them straight. They never tasted great and always had a bitter after bite and they always would stain my fingers. Even the green ones. Nostalgia won over in my mind and I decided that I couldn't keep walking without picking a few.

After a couple minutes down the dirt path, I stumbled upon a little creek and just in front of the creek sat an old log. As I sat on the log I watched as little fish swam downstream. It had been a little while since I came out here, years probably. The ease of going to the overlook paired with the fact that it's between my house and school, meant that I'd nearly forgotten about this creek.

Fortunately for me it was the one place I could go to get away where Zippy surely couldn't find me. I sat for a good fifteen minutes before I heard a giggle. A Zippy giggle. Never can get away.

"Whatcha doin silly boy?"

"Really?" I asked, not even turning around to see the face I already knew I'd see.

"What?"

"Oh Zippy. I guess if I can't beat you I might as well join you."

"Gabe, I'm not too sure I'm following what you're talking about."

"Zippy, I've already told you that I want you to leave me alone. I know you keep telling me that you're an angel but that's just my brain trying to make sense of the figment of my imagination that my tumor has created.

"Oh please, Gabe. Do you have such little faith in anything that you don't believe that there could even possibly be a God looking out for you who loves you enough to send an angel out for you?"

"Not really but if she's going to keep showing up, I might as well give in to her a little."

"You could." She stood behind me. I could feel that she was waiting for me to invite her to join me.

"Come on. I know you want to sit down." I waved her over without even turning around.

She plopped down next to me. She was wearing a white shirt with puffy sleeves, very pirate-esque, and a long flowy lace, baby blue skirt. I looked at her and saw she was gleaming ear to ear.

"Yeah, yeah. Don't think it's so easy now. I'm still not so sure about you, missy."

"Why not?"

I leaned in towards her, grinning, "Well, for starters, I'm the only one who can see you."

"How do you know," she said as she plucked a berry from my hand, "that they can't see me? Maybe they can and this is all just some big joke that everyone's playing on you? Maybe I really am real and I'm just a transfer student?"

I marinated on the possibility for a moment. Of course I have a crazy small group of friends. Then again, who plays a joke that horrible on a kid who has cancer?

"You aren't really considering the possibility, are you?" she asked as she put the berry in her mouth and chewed it. After chewing it she made a twisted face and spit it out, "Oh that's horrible. How are you eating those things?"

"Not too sure. I guess nostalgia is more important than flavor."

"It's not even that they're bad, it's just they go from being beyond sweet to unreasonably bitter. It's odd."

"That sounds a bit like a friend of mine."

"Ha, ha. That's quite horrible to say of me."

"Oh," I said as my face lit up, "You think I was talking about you? Oh nooo Zip. Why of course I didn't mean you."

She stuck her tongue out.

"You just came off so sweet and now it's lies. Lies that my brain made up for me."

"Look at those fish," she said diverting her attention towards the creek.

"What about them?"

"They're just swimming along. Living and breathing. I wonder," she said as she nudged her shoulder against mine, "if they know what purpose they serve."

"Well, they probably don't."

"Why's that?"

"Because, they're fish?"

"Don't think so low of the marine species."

"Zippy, they're little minnows. They're so little they probably only live a few months. Why worry about their place in life?"

"I don't know. Something of the simplicity of them is nice, though, you must admit." She gleamed ear to ear, "Imagine, if you were a little minnow, swimming down the creek."

"Oh, crap."

"What?"

"Do you really think there's something out there that really cares about those little fish? Or even, you know, if something out there is looking down at us talking about us like we're little fish? As if we're just tiny little minnows swimming down a stream unsure of what fate lies ahead of us?"

"I do."

"Of course you do, angel girl."

I watched her as she tried to blow a piece of hair out of her face. Her golden wavy hair was pulled up in a bun and she had one single strand floating around her face. I reached out and gently tucked it behind her ear.

"Why would someone send you to me? Or even care enough to bother? Speaking, hypothetically, that you are indeed real."

"Why do you think?"

I stood up from the log and looked at her, "I give up Zippy. You tell me why."

She stared at me. I picked up a rock and skipped it across the creek.

"Why it is that a little boy loses his dad before he can even get to know the man? Why is it that a recently widowed mom gets raped by a man from the church she's attended for years? Why is it that a fifteen year old girl gets the crap beaten out of her by her jerk ex-boyfriend?" Almost out of breath I added, "Zippy, why is it at fifteen years old I have a severe brain tumor?"

165

Zippy looked at me. Queue the waterworks, "Gabe, I don't know. I don't have the answers for everything that happens in this world. Bad things happen to good people. But they're only bad things if you let them be. If not for the broken moments in our life things would be perfect."

"Personally," I said as I plopped a bitter berry in my mouth, "Perfection doesn't sound too bad at the moment."

"Think about it like this: with perfection, who needs a God? Times of imperfection give us reasons to lean towards the faith of some higher being because we don't have the answers and we aren't perfect, so surely it's easier to put our faith in something greater than ourselves."

"So you're telling me that there's a need for imperfection? A need for flaw simply so that we can look to something higher and know that there is perfection out there but we're not it? Basically, you're saying that we're given these bad, crappy situations to deal with, so we can lean on something bigger than ourselves?"

"I'm not necessarily saying that. But what I am saying is that, well," she chewed on her lip and thought for a moment. "Really, when you think about it there isn't a better time than when you're already beaten and on the ground to look up towards God. You're already on the ground. How much lower can you go? No matter where you look, you're looking up. As far as I'm concerned no matter where I'm looking up from, as long as I look up, I know he's there."

"I see."

"He sent me here to be a blessing to you. You know?"

"How though? How are you possibly going to help me, angel-girl?" I fought back a tear, "Are you going to wipe away this cancer I have? Are you going to bring my dad back to life after ten years?"

"No but I do know that God sent me to you. And he has a path for you but you have to find him. You can't do anything on your own but if you fall into his arms I'm sure he'll guide you to the place where you are supposed to be. Let his light shine through you and be a blessing to this world."

I stared at her in confusion and looked out at the creek, "I just don't know," by the time I looked back at her she'd disappeared.

Just then I heard a rustling of footsteps coming from the trail that leads down to the creek. I looked over my shoulder and saw my mom walking down the trail trying to untangle a twig that had been caught in her hair.

"Hey, you okay? I heard you talking. Thought I'd check on you," She finally unknotted her hair and threw the twig into the creek.

I watched the twig land and create ripples in the current.

I walked closer to where she was standing and we started walking towards the house, "Yeah, I'm fine." As we were walking back through the woods with my mom's arm around my shoulders, I asked her, "Mom, do you believe in angels?"

She stopped and scanned my face, "Well," she said searching my face for reasoning behind the question, then continued walking, "I mean, I haven't given it much thought lately. I suppose once upon a time I did."

We both glanced up the hill and she started giggling.

"Sometimes I like to think that your dad is watching over us. I know it's silly but it's sweet, you know?"

"It's not silly. I think it's neat. Do you think he'd ever, like, shape shift into a teenage girl?"

"I take it you're still seeing the ghost girl that no one sees?"

"Yeah. Only she's not a ghost. She says she an angel."

"Ahhh, I see. No, honestly I can say that I don't think dad would shape shift into a teenage girl. If anything he might would shape shift into, I don't know a tree or something."

"A tree? What kind of fun is that? Who wants to be a tree?"

"I don't know. He was strong and independent but knew how to let the breeze drift through his hair." She rubbed my bald head, "Was your angel the one you were talking to down at the creek?"

"Yeah."

We walked out from the shade of the trees and neared the gate of our backyard.

"What do you talk with her about?" mom asked.

"God. The possibility of one, really."

"I see," she said as she opened the gate.

"Mom, do you believe in God?"

"Come on inside," she said as we walked up the steps to the back door, "We'll have a good talk over breakfast."

●

"Alright, so spill the beans," I said as I sat in one of the wooden chairs at the kitchen table while mom started plating our brunch.

"It's breakfast," she said by the stove with a smirk, "ain't got no beans to spill."

"I mean about your thoughts on God and religion. Like, what's your thought process on the whole shebang?"

"Why all of the sudden are you worried about God, Gabe? Is it the cancer?" She looked over her shoulder at me and I shrugged. "You'll work through it hon."

"Maybe it's not the cancer," I said but after I let the words flow out of my mouth I realized that it possibly was because of the cancer. If it weren't for the cancer I wouldn't have seen Zippy. If I hadn't seen Zippy I wouldn't be asking or even more less thinking, about some God. "I dunno maybe it is the cancer."

She walked over to me and laid down a plate of food. Then she took the seat next to me and rested her head in her hands as she stared at my face, searching for some kind of answer. "What's up? What's going on in that little bald head of yours?"

"A lot," I said as I pushed food around my plate with a fork. "You know how I waved to a girl that you didn't see. Then I had a friend at the hospital that you didn't see leave the room? After that when I was in town and the drug store clerk saw me outside yelling at air?"

She nodded, "That's the angel you were telling me about outside?"

"Yeah, her name is Zippy. Do you think she could really be an angel?"

"I really do hope she is." She said, "We could use an angel around here."

"So you think it's possible?"

"Anything's possible." She said as she stared back at the stove then back to me.

"Do you think that it's just the tumor making me see her?"

"At first when you were talking about your friend and waving to someone I thought you might be going a little looney, especially after the whole thing outside of the drug store. But I really don't know what to think now. I've started questioning things myself."

"You have?"

"Yeah. You know, I'm not one to really like to talk about this but when you were a little boy we would go to church all of the time. Heck, I grew up in the church and had planned on you growing up in the church."

"I know. Why did we stop going?"

She scrunched up her forehead and her tongue floated over her upper teeth, "Ah, well. Ok, you're old enough. Shortly after your dad died I had a," she hesitated, "well, I guess you could call it a 'run-in', with a man from the church. I don't want to go into detail about what happened but after it happened I couldn't find it in me to go back."

"Mom."

"Yeah?"

"I know what happened to you. I just didn't know that was why we didn't go to church anymore. I had my suspicions though."

"Gabe, how could you possibly know? You were practically a baby."

"But I wasn't. I remember crying myself to sleep that night. I remember his gun. I even remember being so scared of everything that night that I climbed into my closet and curled into a ball so that he wouldn't find me. I may not have known what happened then but as I got older I would think back to that and over time I've come to realize what happened to you that night."

My mom inhaled deeply. "Well, now that you know what he did I'll tell you what happened after that event that forced me to not go to church."

"What?"

"There was more of a problem, than what just happened that night, Gabe."

"What? You mean that it wasn't simply that he," I couldn't bring myself to say the word. Rape.

Anger coursed through my veins just knowing that someone had the nerve to use my dad's death as an open opportunity to rape my mother. That she not only had to deal with the death of my father and scramble to figure out how to raise a boy on her own but that she trusted someone to lend a hand and instead he raised his. As if she didn't already have enough on her plate.

"After that day he went home and I guess his wife saw the marks I made from me struggling against him. He told her that I had come on to him."

"You told her the truth though, right!?"

"Gabe, let me continue, please? Anyways, he told her that I had actually come on to him. That I was looking for a shoulder to cry on and that when he told me 'no'and that he wouldn't be," she hesitated, but continued, "intimate with me, that I went bat crazy and started hitting him and scratching him and that's why he had scratches on his neck and his arms."

"Please tell me that you tried to tell them the truth, right?"

"Of course I did. Gosh, it was horrible. The next Sunday at church I couldn't help but overhear all of the whispers. Just the week before people were coming up to me giving me their condolences. That Sunday the women just stared at me. Even the preacher's wife looked at me and I think she raised her eyebrows at me. That woman had some bizarre eyebrows though so I could've just been paranoid."

We sat in silence a few minutes before I looked up at her to see if she was going to go on with the story. She ate a few bites of her brunch and took a swig of her drink.

"After the sermon as I was headed down the outside steps on the way to the car I tried to confront Sarah, the man's wife. I caught her attention and she took off towards her car. I followed after her, with you on my hip. I hated that I had to drag you through that with me but what was I going to do? Leave you on the steps? Or put you in a hot car?"

I shrugged, "I don't know I guess you had to take me with you."

"Well, she finally turned around. When she did she slapped me on the face. I was stunned. 'What the hell is wrong with you', the woman said, 'We tried to help you and you took advantage of my husband like that.' It was amazing to me that this friend of mine, someone I'd grown up with, had believed something so idiotic. I told her what he had done and she looked at me disgusted and said, 'Don't you ever say some crap to me like that'."

"She didn't even believe you for a second? Or give some thought to the possibility?"

"I can't say for sure but I do have my suspicions. After I told her what he did, after she'd slapped me and gossiped about me to the whole congregation, I thought I saw a glimmer in her eyes. As if when I told her that her husband had raped me, she knew that she was in the wrong. If only for a split second, I saw a thought dance past her mind. I think she knew what had really happened. That she'd been naïve to believe her husband when I'd never given her any reason not to trust me. When I was the one who had my husband, who remind you was my high school sweetheart, pass away just two weeks before."

I put a piece of bacon in my mouth, "She didn't say anything about being sorry though?"

"Don't talk with your mouth open. No, she didn't. Right after that she told me never to say anything like that again, turned on her heels, and got in the car."

"That's horrible."

"I know," she scrunched her forehead and let out a sigh of both confusion and relief, "I'm sorry, that was out of line for me to talk to you about."

"Mom, I have cancer, I'll probably die next week anyways. No worries."

"Hush your mouth. You aren't going anywhere. I just know that you have enough to worry about and you don't need something that happened a decade ago to be wearing you down. I've let it wear me down enough on my own."

"But mom," I said as I took her hand, "I needed to know that. I needed to know why it is we don't go to church. I needed to know that it's not just that you don't believe in a god, it's the fact that you were shunned in front of the congregation."

"I do believe in God, Gabe. If it weren't for him I wouldn't be able to put bread on the table. If it weren't for him, situations wouldn't have arisen to let us know that you have cancer. Honestly, I don't think I could have dealt with the fact that you have cancer without losing my sanity without some sense of faith in a higher being. And most of all if it weren't for him I wouldn't have had you in the first place. As long as I have you, my heart is content."

"What happens if you don't have me anymore?"

"I'll have always had you," she said. The look on her face told me that it was something she'd thought about enough and didn't want to think about any more. "But I'm not letting you go anywhere, mister. As for your angel friend, just remember you have a tumor in your temporal lobe. She may be an angel but I wouldn't want you to get your hopes up and her just disappear and never come back once the cancer's gone. I guess as far as whether or not she's an angel, God only knows." She winked and left the table.

●

At chemo that afternoon I sat in the same seat that I usually sit in, surrounded by the same folks I usually sit by. There aren't too many young people running around with cancer where I live. Our town is so small there's only been a cluster of people who have had it, regardless of age. The last person under eighteen to have cancer was five, and she had lymphoma. I've heard stories about her, though I never knew her personally.

Apparently she was spunky. One of the spunkiest kids a person could meet. Any time she was in the hospital doing chemo she'd spend her time making cards. When she'd get done with her session she'd take the cards around to different rooms of the hospital to cheer people up. Of course she wasn't able to write, but her doodles and the fact that she had such a love for life, regardless of her circumstances, made everyone love her.

I'm the youngest out of the group of people who surround me at chemo. The people drift in and out, but for the most part, the gang stays the same.

Ray is a fifty six year old chain smoker. Lung cancer obviously. He had to have a tracheotomy so he could continue to breathe. Whenever he talks he has to press the button the covers the hole in his throat. I like the way he sounds when he does it, gives me something to smile about when sitting in a room filled with dying people.

Ava is a thirty four year old woman with breast cancer. She always wears outfits that you would imagine a housewife from the fifties wearing and always has a matching scarf wrapped around her head. She had to have a mastectomy five years ago, and was in remission until this past July, when they found another lump in her chest area. At first she had trouble with the fact that they'd removed her breast tissue, only for the cancer to come back in other chest tissue.

Then there is Dale. Ohhhhh Dale. Where do I begin with this guy. Dale is sixty years old with testicular cancer that migrated elsewhere to his body. He once played major league baseball and tells me stories about how he enjoyed women waiting for him by the hotel room door during his away games. Even in old age, I couldn't help but notice his strong jaw line and his chiseled facial features. There was no wonder why women loved him. Now he only has one ball. He made sure he told me that the day I met him. He said, "Well you'll be fine. I mean hell, you could have it a lot worse. At least you still have both your balls." I forced a laugh and stared off towards the other side of the room.

Every week it's the same dripping of the IV's, the same chairs, the same people. It really gets tiring having to sit around in a hospital having chemicals dripped into your body. Even worse is the way it makes you feel afterwards. It's a feeling that someone who has not had cancer could never understand.

'Oh, yeah.' They say as they stare at your bald head and your shriveling body, 'I'm sure you must be in a lot of pain'. Well no shit, Sherlock. The crappy thing is it's not even the cancer that's causing the pain but the toxins they shove into your veins to make the cancer 'disappear'. If you're even lucky enough for it to disappear

It seems like a lot of the people who go through chemo are more miserable having to sit through chemo than they would be if they just lived life with cancer. They may not live as long but at least they wouldn't live the last of their days feeling like shit. In theory everyone dies. Whether or not you die today, tomorrow, or ten years from now, you will die. But you aren't dying with toxic sludge coursing through your body. You just are here one moment and gone the next.

Having cancer takes dying to the next level. You're here one day, have cancer the next, and sit in a chair as toxic sludge drips into your body for who knows how long. Ultimately until you die I suppose.

●

Later that night around eight the doorbell rang.

It was my pretty friend. No, not the disastrous one that makes me contemplate the happenings after death but the other disastrous one.

I was lying on the couch trying to watch the T.V. when my mom answered the door. "Well hey! Come on in," she greeted them. "You have company, Gabe."

"Lovely."

They walked into the house looked over at me, my mom and Darla's mom looking somewhat annoyed with what I said.

"He had chemo today," I heard her whisper to the two of them.

"Ahhh," said Darla's mom.

Darla shrugged it off and came and plopped down on the couch next to me.

"What's cookin, good lookin?" she asked with a silly smirk on her face.

"Stomach bile and puke."

"Mmmmmm sounds delicious."

Her mom looked over partially disgusted with Darla's sudden interest in vomit, "I brought some food if y'all are hungry."

"I'm good for now, Mrs. Lively, thank you though," I said.

"It looks delicious," my mom insisted. "How about I get some plates out and we'll eat while we talk about some things."

I looked over the couch, "What kind of things?"

"Don't worry about it. Good things. All good things."

"Why're you being weird?"

"I'm not being weird."

"Would y'all mind if me and Gabe took a little walk first?" Darla asked. "I'm sure Gabe could use some fresh air."

My mom eyed us suspiciously as though she knew what Darla was up to. "Sounds fine to me," she said as she turned to Darla's mom. "How about I make us a cup of coffee while they're out? Then we can eat this delicious food together when they get back. Maybe by then Gabe will be hungry."

"Well," said Mrs. Lively, "I don't suppose that would hurt anyone. As long as you have decaf. If I have anything caffeinated at this time of night, I'll be up for ages."

"Sounds good to me," my mom said as she warmed the oven and put the casserole dishes inside, to keep the food from getting cold. "Cream and sugar?"

"Both please."

We left the house and walked down the gravel driveway. I was walking slightly in front of her and could feel the bits and pieces of gravel biting my ankles from the way she was kicking them up at me when she walked.

She turned around and winked.

"What're you doing that for?"

"Doing what?

"You're purposefully kicking rocks at my legs?"

"Calm down. I was just messing with you." She reached her hand out to me and I took it. We began walking side by side.

Darla nudged her body into me and it nearly knocked me over, "What the hell?"

"Luuuuuucy, you've got some 'splaaaanin to do." Darla said.

"What're you talking about crazy girl?"

"What I'm talking about is why you seem so down in the dumps."

"Aside from you kicking rocks at me and nearly knocking me over?"

"I was just being flirtatious."

"I'm guessing you took a hit of something before you came over for a little walk."

"Nope, I was waiting till I got with my buddy before doing that. You're the one who needs it anyways, not me."

"I don't need it."

"Oh yeah?"

"Yeah," I said sticking my chest out.

"Well, then prove it by going and eating my mom's cooking without puking."

I made a circle in the gravel with my foot, "Meh."

"My thoughts exactly, and she's a killer cook."

"She is. I hated when I had to vomit her stew."

"That must've been....brown."

"Exactly. How long do you think we have?" I asked her.

"I dunno. By the look on your mom's face I assume she could figure out what we're doing."

"I'm sure she does. She caught me and Tony smoking this morning and knew about the other day when you and Tony were over."

"Well she only thinks you smoked this morning, right? It's not like she knows about the other time?"

"Oh, no. Tony left his goodies the other day when both of you were over."

"What?" she said as we continued walking, "He can't be that big of an idiot can he?"

"Oh yeah, he left it right in the open. Said it was a gift but didn't even tell me it was there."

"Yowza. So he came over this morning?"

I nodded.

"Wow, twice in one day? You sure are becoming the little pothead."

"No I'm not. It's just coincidental that you and Tony just happened to stop by on the same day. You guys are the ones who keep bringing that stuff over."

"I'm not so sure if I'd call it coincidence. I'd call it luck," she said with a lift of the eyebrows. "Just because we bring it over doesn't mean that you actually have to smoke."

"Yeah, well." I looked up and saw we were at the overlook.

"We can't just go smoke there with the cars passing by."

"Crap, I didn't really think about it in depth. It's just habitual, you know. My feet led me here." I looked around the area and saw a path walking off in the brush across the road. "Let's go back there."

"Off the side of the road? There's bound to be, like, snakes and stuff in there."

"There are 'like, snakes and stuff' everywhere. Come on."

As we neared the edge of the woods I couldn't help but wonder if I hadn't had cancer would this girl even have given me the time of day. I suppose there really is a God. Maybe he blessed me with cancer so I could spend time with this angel on earth.

Yeah right.

"How was chemo?" she asked as she walked over a fallen tree.

"Oh you know, the usual. Wonderful. There's a clearing right over here." I walked a little bit further into the woods and sat down on a patch of grass. I took my hoodie off and laid it out beside me. "Come sit on this."

"I'll be fine sitting on the grass, I don't want your hoodie to get dirty."

"Well it's either my hoodie or your clothes, and personally I'd prefer my hoodie get dirty. Your mom would be mad if you came back to my house with dirt all over you."

"'What did those kids do on their walk'," she said as her eyes lit up. "So your day was good?"

"Oh yeah. I just love sitting in a chair for hours as poison seeps into my veins. Especially when I had the chance to sit next to other people I have nothing in common with."

"Well," she said as she smoked, "Now you're here with me. So that makes it all better. Right?" She passed and I took it.

"Right." I agreed. How could I not agree with her? I mean does she not realize that I've been waiting around since I was nine years old to have her sitting next to me at her own free will? I'm sure she does.

"Okay pretty boy. I have a question for you."

"Shoot."

"Why do you love me?" she made a shooting gesture with her hands, "Bang Bang." She asked with a straight face.

The question startled me, "Who said I love you?"

"I did. And you do. Don't try and deny it. You've loved me since fourth grade. I'm just curious why." She started laughing hysterically, "You've always been beyond sweet to me and always had a thing for me. I'm just not sure why. I mean any guy who puts some creepy bug on a girl's desk has to have a thing for her. Right?"

My mouth fell open.

"Come on, you had to know I knew it was you who brought the bug in."

"But Tony told everyone it was him?"

"Gabe, you were always playing with bugs. I always had my suspicions but now I know it was you. So, tell me of this long aficionado for little old Darla."

"Well," I said as I scooted over towards her, "You're kind. You're sweet," I shrugged.

"Come on, Gabe. It has to be something a little bit more than that. Give me some depth. I know you've got depth to you. I feel it every time you're around."

"You're warm," I continued as I wrapped my arms around her. "The minute you enter a room you make everyone feel warm. As if nothing else is going on. The world stops and all of the cameras turn to you. You're simply amazing." In that moment I made a bold attempt to kiss her. I held her head in my hands and kissed the girl of my dreams, "And holy crap you always smell like cocoa butter. It's like you lather up in the stuff."

My mind wandered and I imagined Darla dancing in a pool of cocoa butter. Throwing it up in the air and smothering herself with the stuff.

"I've always liked it. It's almost chocolaty but not quite. Kind of makes me think of the beach too."

"Yeah. Man, I could definitely go for some chocolate cookies."

"My mom brought fudgy chocolate brownies over."

"Really?" my mouth was watering.

"Oh yeah, the good kind too. Homemade, and just so gooey. She even added a layer of caramel in between."

"How the heck do you get a layer of caramel in the brownies? Like wouldn't it all melt?"

"Nah," she said as she leaned her head on my shoulder. "She bakes two pans of brownies, then when they've cooled off she puts a layer of caramel on top of one and sits the other pan of brownies on top of the caramel. They're amazing."

"That sounds killer right about now."

Darla leaned into me and started tracing the edges of my lips with her finger, "I just love the edge pieces of the brownie. They're all gooey, but then on the side they're all…crunchy."

Darla put her hands at the nape of my neck and closed her eyes as she drew in to a kiss.

"See," she said as she leaned away, her eyes meeting mine, "I knew you loved me."

"Why are you so sure?"

"You closed your eyes when we kissed. You only close your eyes when you kiss someone you love."

"So your eyes were open then? So it's a one way street isn't it?"

"I didn't say that. It's possible that I just opened my eyes right before you opened yours."

"Ah," I rubbed my jaw line.

"Don't be silly or getting all weird on me. You know I've always loved you, not just 'as a friend', either."

"Really?"

"Oh, yeah. Man, Jake knew it too. That's why he pitched such a fit that day I was coming back to school from making you breakfast."

"You didn't tell him we kissed though? Did you?"

"I didn't have to. He knew that even for me to be over there taking care of you that it was over between us."

"He knew the whole time that you cared about me, didn't he?"

"Of course he did. He knew that my relationship with him was only skin deep. That he was lacking something that you have. He was a total jerk who would never let me in. He knew he could never have the heart and soul like you do and even though we were just friends and I never told him anything about having feelings for you he could feel it. Everyone could feel it."

"I can feel it." I told her as I resumed kissing her under the trees.

"Gabe, we should probably get back to your house."

"You're right." I stood up and helped her off of the ground. I put my hoodie on her shoulders to keep her warm.

●

We walked back to my house hand in hand. Her's were soft and had nails that were painted pink with little yellow flowers on the tips. Little

Darla Lively's hand placed in cancer ridden Gabe Perkins' hand.

I knew I'd love her for the rest of my life. I opened up the screen door to the house and we walked in hand in hand and our moms turned and looked at us. Both of them were blushing and giggling.

"Welcome back love birds," said my mom. "Hope you two didn't get into too much trouble."

"I hope you didn't either," Mrs. Lively said cautiously.

Darla ran over and hugged her mom, "No trouble here, momma. It smells amazing in here."

"That's your mom's food being warmed up in the oven," said my mom, "It's been in there as long as yall've been gone. Which has been about an hour or so now."

"Sorry, mom," I said as I walked into the kitchen. "We didn't think we'd have such a long walk. We're back now though and I'm starving," I turned my attention to Darla's mom. "Darla told me about these amazing brownies you brought over, and I honestly can't wait to sink my teeth into a few of them."

"Well," my mom said as she stood up from the table and made her way into the kitchen, "You need to eat some real food first."

Darla's mom went into the kitchen to help my mom get everything unwrapped. "Y'all come on over and make a plate and we'll all have a talk."

"Sure," I said. I looked over to Darla to see if her face would tell what kind of talk this would be and she shrugged. We all grabbed a plate of food and sat down at the dinner table together.

"So," I started, "what's there to talk about?"

"Well," said my mom, as she took a swig of sweat tea, "You remember how we talked about doing a fundraiser?"

"Yeah, of course."

"That's why we came over, Gabe." Mrs. Lively said, as Darla looked at me and took my hand. "If you're up to it we'd like to start a fundraiser for you. On a much larger scale than we originally thought we'd do."

"Really?" I said as my heart danced around inside of me.

"Yeah," said Darla getting excited. "When my mom came to me to talk to me about helping out with a fundraiser I was thinking that we could have like this carnival at the store we have in town. You know, dunking booth, little rides, some games. And all the profits could go to your medical bills."

"That sounds like it could be cool," I said as I picked up a biscuit that was laced with gooey flaky layers and butter oozing from a cut in the middle.

"Definitely," said Mrs. Lively. "I got to talking to some friends of ours and the owners of the old fair grounds said that they'd like to host it."

"I get my own fair!" I turned my attention to Darla, with potatoes stuffed in my cheeks, "Darla! I get to have my own fair."

Her eyes widened and she reached over and cupped her hand in front of my mouth. I pulled my lips together as she retracted her hand.

"Oh, sorry," I said with a swallow.

"Yes, you'd get to have your own fair, Gabe," said Darla as she giggled.

"We'd like to even have a fund going in our other stores around the area. You know like maybe having little jars at the checkout line. It may not bring in as much as the fair but it could help offset whatever the fair didn't cover."

"Is there going to be a ferris wheel?"

"That may cost more money than it would actually bring in, Gabe," my mom said.

"Well, actually the company that we're renting some booths from may give us a little wiggle room. I had contacted them about some of their game booths and they'd match our costs. So let's say we spent a thousand dollars on renting a booth, they'd give us another thousand dollars to spend on renting other booths."

"That's wonderful," my mom said.

"I really appreciate all that y'all are willing to do to help out. It means more than I can even express." I stuffed my face with a tuna noodle dish and another roll. "Oh my gosh, thank you for bringing dinner over. It's amazing. Mom, you have to learn how to make this stuff, it's all cheesy and melty in my mouth. I just love it."

"Gabe," said Mrs. Lively, "Are you alright?"

"Trust me," I said pointing to my food and then my mouth, "I'm beyond alright, thanks to you."

My mom squished her eyes together, as if doing so would make my mental state come back down to normal. "Yes, Lou, you'll have to give me the recipe," she said as she pressed her fingers on her temples.

"Darla, your mom's name is Lou? That's so cool. My dad's name was Lou. Almost, it was like Louuuu-kuh. See, it's just another sign for us."

"Actually," Darla's mom said curiously, "it's LouAnne, but people just call me Lou."

"I like it."

"Well," said Darla, switching the gears of the conversation, "I'm glad you're up for the fair, you know? I really was worried that you wouldn't want all the attention."

"As long as you're there to steal some of the attention from me I'll be fine." We made googly eyes and our moms just stared.

"So, Sheila," Mrs. Lively said trying to divert her attention away from us making lovey faces at each other, "when do you think it would be a good day for us to go ahead with the fundraiser?"

"Well, how much time do you think you'll need to pull things together?" my mom asked."

"I was thinking that two months should be enough time to get the different booths booked up for, and to have enough time to get the word around town. The beginning of November?"

"Sounds like a plan. What do you think Gabe?"

I turned my focus away from Darla and over to my mom. "I think that sounds like a great idea."

We finished dinner and Darla and I went outside to talk on the front porch as our moms started planning on the fundraiser.

"Hey, Darla," I said to her as I looked up at the stars in the sky. Not a cloud in the sky. They twinkled as if a thousand little diamonds had been tossed into the air.

"Hey, Gabe," she replied.

"What do you think about angels?"

She looked at me curiously and then asked, "What do you mean?"

"Well, I mean, what do you think about angels? Do you think they're real? Or even, like, you know God? I'm not really sure about it all. I mean, I've never given it too much thought but ever since I found out I had cancer I've started wondering."

"I think there's definitely a God," she said without an ounce of hesitation.

"What about angels?"

"Maybe. Are you still seeing your angel girl?"

"Yeah. I keep seeing her. I've kind of began to give in to the idea that she's going to be around regardless of whether I want her to be or not."

"Well there you go, the proof is in the pudding."

"So you think she's real?"

"Maybe but then again I think that if she were really an angel instead of something your head was making you see, wouldn't she leave you alone after you asked a few times? I mean, I know personally if someone were to tell me to leave them alone I would. Visions don't have that level of realness to leave someone alone."

"Oh, please. You wouldn't leave someone alone if they threw you off a cliff. You'd just start climbing the rock wall until you were with them again."

"What makes you think that?"

"Hello, don't you remember me yelling at you in the boys bathroom at school?"

"Ahhh, yes. Now I remember. Well I guess if your angel girl is anything like me she may have a problem leaving you alone."

She leaned her head on my shoulder and I wrapped my arms around her. I inhaled and the smell of her shampoo slinked through my nostrils. It smelled like hazelnut butteryness. If her hair smelled so good, would it taste good too? I licked it to see. Nope. Tasted like hair.

Darla pulled away, "Did you just lick my head?"

"No," I said as I wiped my tongue off with the back of my hand. "You just smell like chocolate. Can you really blame me?" BROWNIES. "I forgot about your mom's brownies."

"I'll go grab some," she said she stood up.

I couldn't help but stare at her butt as she got up. Darla was tiny, I could probably put my hands around her waist and my fingers would touch, but for a skinny girl, she had a bubble butt. Not a jiggley one, but one that looked like a capital letter 'B' turned sideways.

Darla came back out with a bowl filled with brownies. They looked as delicious as she had described them to be. The brown caramel dripped over the crevices of the fudgy brownie bits.

"Ahhh, my wench has brought me treasure."

She glared at me, "Just eat one."

I put one in my mouth, "Ohhhh my God!" The brownie melted in my mouth as my teeth bit into random chunks of chocolate. Caramel gushed out from between my teeth and shot into my cheek as I savored the delicious balance of salty and sweet. "Your mom has a gift, Darla. These are killer."

"Man, I wish I had that effect on you."

"Trust me," I said with a wink. "You do."

"So," I said as I got my train of thought back. I licked the corner of my mouth to get some of the caramel that had dribbled out, "What's your thought on God."

"I definitely think there's some higher power out there."

"Really? But what makes you so sure? I mean, for me, eating these brownies were a sure enough sign."

"Gabe," she said giggling. She got closer to me and leaned on my shoulder and motioned her hands out to the world around us, "we live in the mountains. There are beautiful sights everywhere. Your favorite overlook for instance," she looked at me and I nodded. "How do you explain that something so beautiful could be a mistake? That everything beautiful in the world, the trees, the mountains, the oceans, me and you, how could all that just randomly appear. That it just is happenstance that these amazing things are on this Earth and that we're somehow here to explore it. I think it's a lackluster idea to believe for a second that there isn't a God. In any form, it just makes sense that there's something out there that created us. I think dismissing the idea is just an easy way out."

"So what religion are you?"

"I'd say Christian. I definitely feel a connection to it. I'm not a push my ideals down your throat kind of Christian but the kind who thinks that there is definitely someone out there looking out for us. I mean, how wonderful is it that there could be a God out there who cares enough about us to let his son come to earth just to die for us? It's beautiful, you know?"

"Sounds bizarre to me. Guess what son? Get down to Earth and die for everyone around you who have led crappy lives even though you were perfect. Go die for them."

"That makes it even more awesome of an idea that it happened."

"Maybe."

"Yes," she looked just above my lip for a second. "You have a couple brownie crumbs," she leaned in as if she was going to kiss me, but instead of a puckering, she sucked the chocolaty brownie bits off of my upper lip. "All gone."

"Mmm."

"I mean how many people can you say you know that are like 'hey you! I love you so much that in thirty years my son is going to die for your soul'. It's just deep."

"Yeah. Deep."

"But I mean I know not everyone is going to have the same beliefs as me and that's understandable. The only thing I can't understand are people who believe there's nothing out there. Personally I think it takes more faith to believe in nothing than to believe in something."

"You're a pretty smart girl."

"Yeah, but I can't take credit for that line."

"Then who can?"

"Einstein." She continued in a well-articulated accent, "I do believe, 'twas Einstein who once said 'It takes more faith to believe in nothing, than to believe in something." She dropped the accent. "And you know, Einstein was kind of a genius." She winked, "I just think I wouldn't have the balls to discount everything that I've seen throughout my life, good or bad, to be deemed 'accident' or 'just there'. It just seems silly."

"I guess so. But do you think your God could send us angels?"

"Oh this again," she leaned back against my shoulder, and actually took a moment to think on it. "Sure why not, I mean I've never seen an angel. But I think it's possible. I think if God cared enough about us to let his son die for us then why wouldn't he care enough about us to send angels to watch over us. I'm not too sure how it would work out, but I wouldn't be surprised if they've intervened in situations a time or two."

I got quiet for a minute and I could feel the tension in the air.

"You don't have anything to worry about. I know you're a little freaked out by everything but you'll be fine. Ok?"

I think she wanted me to reassure her that I would be okay. She wanted me to look at her and say 'Yes, Darla, everything's going to be ok.' I so badly wanted to.

I shrugged and nodded.

"Ohhhhh," she started singing. "My liiitttle angel boy."

"Shh. I've talked to my mom about it and she's coming around to the idea of my angel friend

197

but I think she's still skeptical. Thinks I'm going a little nutso."

"Why would she think that?"

"Because," I continued with my version of Darla's articulated accent, "my tumor is large and is pressing on my temporal lobe." I hesitated and continued with my own tone of voice, "I had seen the angel twice before we found out what kind of cancer it was and she mentioned it to the doctor and he said that it could be a hallucination caused by my tumor pressing on my temporal lobe. Apparently other people who have had anaplastic ogligodendroglioma near their temporal lobe have had hallucinations. It's somewhat of a symptom."

She looked at me then at the ground, "Nope. You saw an angel, Gabe." She had been convinced. She jumped up with a burst of energy as if she was going to do a cartwheel, looked back at me, and continued, "See! That's an easy way out. One of science's many easy ways out. Write off seeing an angel as a hallucination."

"Think so? I mean, not even twenty minutes ago you were questioning it."

"Yeah, but I've changed my mind. I was being too logical, and in life there are so many things that can't be described through logic. I mean you tell me. Like, how many times have you seen her?"

"A lot. Right before I found out I had cancer, countless times after."

"Then don't write it off as a hallucination."

"You know what I don't want to write off as a hallucination?"

"What?"

"This. This whole, you and me thing."

"I'm not sure I know what you're talking about."

"Darla, I want to be your boyfriend."

"Gabe," she said as her eyes twinkled and her cheeks grew pink, "You already are my boyfriend." She leaned down and kissed my head.

# Chapter 7

After Darla and her mom left I sat on the front porch for a while. It wasn't much of a porch, more of a stoop. It was my stoop. I had wide open skies to stare out at and a few back porches and clothing wires to stare back at me.

Thoughts began rambling through my head. Mainly thoughts about Darla. She was always a friend of mine but more in a Santa being friends with the misfit toys kind of way. To finally have her as my girlfriend is really all that I've ever dreamed of. I suppose a dying man's last wish has been fulfilled.

Could it even possibly be the simple fact that I am a dying boy that has drawn her closer to me? What would Darla have to lose if she dated a boy who had cancer, that she knew was going to die, and he died. For all I know it could be a play of sympathy just an extreme dose of sympathy that she handed over to poor little old cancer ridden me. I would hate that. Hate that with a vengeance.

It would be more of a princess finding a bird with a broken wing, trying to nurse it to health, only for it to die. The princess wouldn't wilt and die herself, but she'd move on and find more birds to fix until she found herself a prince. My Darla, fixing her bird.

"What's up Gabey Baby?" my mom said as the screen door shut behind her and she brought me back from a daze.

"Nothing really." After a pause wondering whether or not to let my mom into my heart, I finally let it go, "Mom. Why do you think Darla has all the sudden taken an interest in me?"

"Because she's always had an interest in you," she said.

"I always saw her as the pretty girl who was just being nice."

"Gabe, allow me to let you in on a little secret will you?" She looked for approval, I nodded, and she continued. "No one truly does anything to just 'be nice'."

"I see it happen all the time."

"Alright, well look at it from this perspective" Why in the world would a girl like Darla who has everything in the world going for her from looks to grades, allow you to stumble on her path and let her emotions get trampled on?" I shrugged and she continued, "A girl like Darla, who as sweet as she may be could date any boy she wanted to, yet she has always felt connected to you. And now she's finally opening up to let you see how she truly feels."

"Because of the cancer mom. It's because of the cancer."

"Gabe, I can tell you right now that it's not. Someone might think that 'oh it's an easy way out to like a boy with a brain tumor'. But guess what?

It's not. Could you possibly imagine what she has to constantly think about? She's putting herself on a ride with you, which may end short. She's allowing herself to be opened up to someone who for all she knows may not be there in the next year."

"Well jeez mom that makes me feel better."

"You will be here, Gabe. I'm just trying to make you understand from her point of view. Honestly, if you ask me, I wouldn't be surprised if she cared for you ever since that whole lollipop thing."

"Oh my Gooood!" I threw my hands up in the air. "If I have to hear about that lollipop thing one more time…"

"Calm down. Anyways, I think if your tumor is to blame for anything it's for waking Darla up and making her realize that life is short. So short that she couldn't sit around and let her feelings for you go unnoticed. She wanted to let you see how much she cared for you. If anything the cancer has led her to you not because of an easy way out or because you'll 'die anyway so what does it matter', but because she doesn't want to waste what precious time she has with you now."

"I guess so."

"Well stop guessing so, and respect her time, and get to knowing so."

"She's a pretty phenomenal girl."

"I know that son," she said and began to get up to go inside.

Right when she reached the door, I blurted out, "I talked to Darla about God tonight."

Mom turned and came down the stairs to me. "Oh, you did huh?"

"Yeah, I did, she was actually pretty enthusiastic about it all."

"Really, now?"

"Yeah, apparently she's a Christian. Not like a pushy judgmental one, but like, she actually really believes in it all. I guess I never really gave any thought to her having faith in anything."

"Probably because you two are just now getting close."

"I guess. I also talked to her about angels."

"Oh, lordy. Again with the angel girl."

"I can't help it, I just see her. I tell her to go away and I see her."

"You see her often?"

"Not all the time, but on occasion."

"You know, it's a nice thought that something could be watching over you. I do have to admit though that it makes me worry about you, in a bad way."

"You always have worried about me."

"Yeah, but now it's a more in a more deeply rooted way."

Her worry for me made me worry about myself.

"Darla believes in angels. Not that she's seen them or anything. But it's beautiful, like she believes it's possible. She thinks that there's a chance that I'm not fully insane. Mom, she even said that it's an easy way out to discount my angel as just a hallucination from my brain tumor."

"Alright, well think about this my way. It would be one thing if you were seeing angels and you didn't have a tumor that was sitting in the exact position that a tumor that causes hallucinations sits, but you are and you do. You have the exact kind of tumor that causes hallucinations, Gabe. Can't you see why it would be easy for me to think that it was the cancer making you see her?"

"I could possibly understand it, but can't you just believe for two seconds, please just believe with me here, that I could be seeing an angel?"

I lingered for her to say something. I could feel the tension in the air pressing down on me.

"I love you, Gabe, but you have anaplastic cancer. That means it's deadly, so when something that's known to be a side effect of the cancer comes to light, it worries me. I'm worried. You're my son. I've already lost your father, do you know what it would do to me if I lost my baby too?"

"Well wake up, mom." I said as I stood up. "Chances are that you just might."

I got up and left. I wandered. As I wandered I could hear her screaming after me. To come back, that she was sorry for hurting me. But I was tired. Too tired of seeing how hurt my mom was. How hurt my mom was because of the fact that I was dying. I was killing my mom and my body was killing me.

●

I was beyond drained but went on a trek through the woods. Walking seemed like the only thing best for me to do. The only thing I really could do to blow what little steam I had left off. Past the creek, down a hill and out the other side of the woods. Rather than going the beaten path down to my overlook, I went through the jungle. The same place I'd sat with Darla not even a few hours ago.

I looked both ways before trotting over to the lookout, just to be sure a car didn't kill me before the plague of a disease that was being stored in my brain could.

While I was there I stared out into the open skies. I stood anxiously, waiting for a shooting star that I could wish on to fly by. But my shooting star never came. Tears poured down my face while I hoped that one would shoot by. If I could just set my eyes upon that one shooting star and wish, it would all be better. Maybe, just maybe I could see that intangible star and for a second I could believe that if I wished on it that all of my troubles would be gone. I'd even be happy with an airplane. I could pretend it was a star. It would look close enough like a star and I could convince myself it was one.

When most people my age see a shooting star I would imagine that they wish something of the likes of being allowed to go to a party or sharing a kiss with the pretty girl. Not me though, no not Gabe Perkins. Through some horrible game of chance, during my year of being fifteen, life had dealt me a hard card to handle. One that would make me not only wish upon a shooting star but wish upon the idea and hope for a shooting star. So that I could wish upon a star as a dying dreamer would.  I held my face in my hands as the tears kept pouring.

I was up here where no one could hear me up here but the birds and squirrels, "Why, me?" I asked an empty valley, "Why did this happen to me? " At this point I was hoping for an answer from a Godly being. "My God," I shouted, "Why would you do this to me? What have I done that was so bad!?"

I felt a pair of arms wrap around and hold me. I knew in that moment I wasn't hallucinating, I was feeling the warmth and love of an angel. An angel who was sent to me because I had someone out there who cared so much for me, to send an angel to comfort me through having a cancer ridden body.

"Gabe," whispered Zippy, "everything is going to be okay. He has you in the palm of His hand and He knows what He is doing."

"Why though? Why should I have to go through something like this? I'm only fifteen. More importantly why is it that other kids, the ones younger than me have to go through this? Kids who have a life that's barely even started? Shouldn't someone have to experience life before they experience death?"

"You're not dead though," she said as I laid my head on her shoulder. "More importantly everyone dies. It's not the longevity of a life that matters, rather the quality of a life you live in the time you're here. God has a plan for everyone and everything. He has a time for beginning and a time for ending. He has a purpose for everyone's life. He has a plan for you Gabe. He knows what he's doing and while it may seem horrific that someone your age should have to face the possibility of death, His timing is best."

"I just feel so hopeless, Zippy. There's really nothing I can do."

"You know sometimes the best time to reach out to God is when you do feel hopeless. Stop worrying about things so much. Why worry about how long you have left to live when you have no control over it?"

"Well if I'm not going to worry about it who is?"

Zippy pulled away from me, smiled and pointed up, "Stop spending your precious time worrying about it and let someone who can actually fight this worry about it."

"But how am I supposed to give up the pain that goes with dealing with this?" I asked as I rubbed my tears away with the sleeve of my hoodie.

"Give it up to Him. Pray and just tell Him that you know what? You can't deal with it anymore. All the things that come along with it, you can't handle it, so you tell Him you want Him to lift it off your shoulders."

"Then....?"

"And then you stop thinking about it. You let His business be His business. Let Him deal with it because you can't. Gabe, there's nothing you can do about it. You go to chemo right?"

"Oh yes."

"Okay, you're doing all you can. Let Him do His job and let yourself be done with it," She lifted brushed her hands together, pulled them apart, and shrugged.

"That's one load off but it's not even just about the cancer anymore."

"Oh, Gabe. Come on. Stop throwing yourself this pity party. It's hard to be around you like this."

"Zippy, you do realize that if I told people I was talking to an angel that the majority of them would think I was crazy. Or worse, they'd think that my cancer probably was getting worse and would think you're just a side effect."

She rubbed her shoulder and twisted away in denial, "Oh, please, it's not that bad."

"Zippy, the majority of people would think I'm bonkers if I told them I talk to angels. In fact, I can guarantee it, as the majority of people I have actually told have thought I was insane."

"Well, you said the majority of them, not all of them," she reasoned.

I looked down at the stone wall and picked up a piece of rock and tossed it out in front of me. Would anyone notice if someone threw a rock from way up here? Would it set off a domino effect? Or would it just land somewhere, uncharted to anyone around it?

I looked up and as I had guessed, she was gone.

"That woman," I mumbled. Wait. Are angels women? Of course, she looks like one, but how can you tell a female from a male angel. Female angels would be more appealing in my head. At least to have to be around and gain comfort from. Men have never really been comforting to me. I'm not too sure what I would have thought of Zippy if she were a male.

The angel of death would probably have to be a guy, though. I mean, think about it if some big aura of a muscular man came up to me and said 'Let's go, NOW!' I'd probably want to run and hide, but I'd be more afraid of what he'd do if I didn't go with him.

Then again if the angel of death were a woman, she could lure people off to heaven, or wherever their final destination was. People wouldn't want to run and hide. They'd be all, 'Oh yes, I'll follow you wherever you take me'.

I sat there reflecting over everything that's happened in since school started. I've gone from the extremes of being a happy healthy young guy to being a frail weak cancer ridden creature that resembles the likes of a hobbit. I've gone from being some weird creepy kid with no social life, to a weird creepy kid with a girlfriend and an angel watching over him. Err, maybe it hasn't been such a bad thing.

It would've never passed my thoughts five months ago that I would be sitting here deteriorating. At the same time I would've never thought that I'd be dating the girl of my dreams. If it took cancer to take me to the point where I have Darla then I guess that's OK with me. I'd rather be alive for seven more days and have the chance to express my feelings for her, rather than live seventy more years and never get the chance to run my fingers through her brown hair. Death and Darla seem more beneficial for me than a life without her.

I traveled home slower tonight than I would any other night. Kicking rocks along the way while thinking about what life would be like without the cancer. No more chemo. No more creepy old people to sit around while having an IV drip toxic fluid into my blood stream.

The thought that kept creeping up in the back of my head was also one that I was sure of. Without the cancer there probably would be no Darla.

Sometimes in life we never get to really say what we feel for one another because we have this strange mentality that there will always be another day, and another opportunity to express our feelings. When someone comes into the awareness of the fact that they have a terminal illness, it frees the padlocks that we have over our own hearts and emotions. It allows us to pull whatever it is in our guts and spill them on the table, not giving a damn what anyone thinks about it.

Because there may not be a tomorrow.

In reality, who's to say that anyone will have a tomorrow? I may have been given a time limit on how long I could live, yet for all John Doe knows, he could walk to his car, hop in and go for a ride, only to be hit head on by someone grabbing something out of the floorboard of their passenger seat. No one truly knows the extent to which they will carry on living.

To this realization I began to wonder, is it really me who has the lower hand? And that those around me living out healthy lives the upper hand? Or is it that given my state and knowledge, that I've been given the upper hand simply because I have to live in a state of full expression of my feelings or I could die tomorrow with no one ever really knowing how I felt towards them.

I couldn't bare the guilt I felt for the emotional damage I'd probably laid thick on my mom earlier in the night. As I dragged my feet up the driveway, I made sure to walk towards my bedroom window to avoid her curled up in the corner of the couch, probably drenched in tears. I pushed a patio chair over to the window and attempted opening it. Opening a window that had been locked from the inside proved more difficult than one could imagine, especially if you were under the impression that it was still unlocked.

I hopped off of the chair and walked around the house back to the front door. Opening the front door can also be fairly difficult if the door is locked. I knocked on the door and yelled for my mom with the hopes that she would open it. When she didn't open the door I put my forehead to the glass to peek in to see if she might've fallen asleep on the couch. She wasn't on the couch, and all the lights in the house were off. My mind began to scramble trying to figure out where she'd gone. The only place I could think of where she may have went to was the Lively's house. My mom didn't have many friends but through the cancer and mine and Darla's relationship, our mothers had rekindled their old friendship.

After waking up at six in the morning to find my friend standing outside, having to deal with chemo, having dinner with Darla and her mom, I was drained. Add to that going nuts on my mom and having to go on a wild goose chase for her, meant the wearing down of an already worn out mind.

The doorbell was bright and shiny, but I liked their door knockers better. Something about the fact that not every door had door knockers, made them that more impressive. After a couple knocks Darla's dad came down and answered the door.

After he rubbed the fog off of his glasses he noticed it was me, "Oh hey there Gabe," he said as he munched on a gooey caramel brownie, "It's pretty late for you to be out isn't it?"

"Yes sir," I said as I stared at the ground, "but I'm looking for my mom. I kinda took off from the house earlier after getting into an argument with her." And then it hit me that I was telling my girlfriend's dad about an argument I had with my mom. What kind of kid will he think I am if I sit around having arguments with my mom and then take off into the woods? A pretty screwed up one I guess.

Nail on the head.

"I'm sorry it's late and I shouldn't have come here." I started to head off and as I walked away Darla's dad stopped me.

"Gabe, wait." I turned back to him and he continued, "You're mom and my wife went to the diner for some coffee. I assumed you would've known. Then again I guess you taking off had probably been the reason they went out in the first place. If you want I can run you by there?"

"That would be great."

"Alright let me just grab my keys and a coat and we'll go."

Darla's dad went back inside and came out wearing his housecoat and slippers. "I don't plan on getting out, so don't mind the attire." We walked to his car and got in. Once we buckled up he held out a napkin with a brownie on it, "Lou made these. They're delicious."

I happily took the brownie from him and held back the urge to gobble it down, "I know sir, she brought some over this afternoon, they were amazing, I must admit. Thank you for taking me."

"It's no problem. Sorry that Darla's not with us, she's already asleep."

"No, I understand completely. I'm just glad you're taking me to mom."

"No problem kid."

We arrived at the diner and my mom was sitting in a booth with Mrs. Lively. Mom's face was puffy and swollen and she had mascara stains dripping down her cheeks, reminiscent of Harley Quinn.

She looked up at me and quickly looked down at the table, using the back of her hands to wipe away any of the mascara residue that may've fell down her face. She looked back at me and said, "There you are. I've been worried about you.

"I'm fine. I just went to the overlook."

"I wasn't so much about where you were, but just about you."

"I'm sorry, mom."

"You can't just run off like that anymore, Gabe. I can't handle it. A few months ago it wouldn't have mattered and I could've written it off as you just behaving like a teenage boy. But now, it's more than that. You're my son and I'm your mother."

"I know mom."

"Don't cut me off. You're fighting a much bigger battle than most kids your age. And it's not just you who's fighting that battle. Everyone around you is carrying that weight too. It's ten times more painful for me to deal with your attitude now, than it was before I knew you had cancer."

"I understand."

"No. You don't, Gabe. If you did you wouldn't have run off. I can't handle you doing that anymore. Not only are you reckless with your actions but you're reckless with your emotions." She turned to Mrs. Lively, "I'm sorry you have to hear all of this."

"If you want I can go and you and Gabe can sit."

"No, you're fine, Lou."

"Gabe, you need to straighten up. I'm already on an emotional roller coaster and I can't handle the extras. Stop bringing the drama to your momma." She turned her attention to Darla's mom, "Thank you so much Lou for coming here with me. I know you have a family at home to take care of," she said more to me than Lou, "but it meant the world for me to have an old friend bare this with me. We're going to go ahead and head home for the night, but thank you so much."

"You know my door's always open if you need me."

She gave Darla's mom a hug and took me by the shoulder and we walked out.

The whole car ride home my mom was silent. Even as she got out of the car she didn't say anything to me. It's one thing when a parent is so angry that they yell at you, but being given the silent treatment? Way scarier.

●

Trying to sleep that night was like trying to slay a dragon with my finger. Pointless. I tossed and turned the entire night, to no avail. Even waking up in the morning was fairly pointless to try to do. I kept trying to go back to sleep but no matter how much I rolled around in the sheets I was never going to get rest. I finally dragged myself out of bed and walked out into the small hallway to the living room.

My mom was putting her coat on and heading out the door. I ran up to her and gave her a huge hug.

"I'm sorry about last night mom. I really am," I told her.

"I know you are and it's OK. I'm scheduling an appointment with Dr. Weiss A.S.A.P."

"Why? I just went to chemo yesterday?"

"You've been more moody than normal."

"I'm a teenage boy going through puberty. That's normal."

"Well, maybe there's something they can give you for it. Maybe you've just been depressed since you've found out you have cancer."

"I don't want to be on even more medication mom."

"Gabe, I just have this overwhelming feeling in my gut that something isn't right. Call it mother's instinct, call me crazy, call it what you will, but you need an appointment with him. Maybe just a CT scan to prove that there isn't anything going on and that I'm just a crazy worried mom."

"You're worried because I'm so sure of the fact that I see an angel, aren't you?"

Her posture slumped and she took a deep sigh before finally looking up at me. "She may be an angel for all I know, but what if it is something bigger than that? I really can't help but wonder if chemo's really doing anything for you. You're still having hallucinations, you know?"

"You may think she's a hallucination but I know she's real."

"Then let's just go to Dr. Weiss and let him tell us that himself. Let him tell us that you're tumor is shrinking and that your friend couldn't possibly be a hallucination. Let's even pretend that your moodiness is because of your age, rather than the cancer."

She kissed me on the head and left for work.

Later in the afternoon she called me to tell me that she had set up an appointment for the next day. I'm not quite sure what would freak me out more, the fact that I actually have been talking to an angel, or the fact that we've been pouring toxic sludge into my veins all in vain.

Would it make me discount anything that Zippy had told me? About a bigger picture, and a higher being who loved me?

●

Twelve in the afternoon. Most people would be eating lunch around this time. Me? Oh no, the thought would be too puke provoking. Instead I was sitting in the waiting room at the local hospital waiting to have a nice little visit from Dr. Weiss. We did my CT scan yesterday and he called us in to have a nice little chat.

Why do they always have you come in to talk with them? Can't they tell you the guts of the story over the phone? But then again, letting a person down over the phone is frowned upon, isn't it?

My mom walked up to the counter and checked me in.

A door next to the check in counter opened and an older nurse with a friendly, toothy smile greeted us, "Gabe Perkins."

We got up and headed towards the door. She led us down the hall to a little room, in which we'd wait probably another thirty minutes for the doctor. "How've you guys been?" she asked as we walked down the hallway.

"We've been doing good, thanks," replied my mom.

"That's good to hear. You guys just hang tight in here and Dr. Weiss will be with you shortly."

"Thank you," said my mom.

For some reason I was lacking the want to talk to people today. Not that I ever really cared to in other situations but today I just felt heavy. Leaden with emotions and not interested in anything anyone else had to say. I couldn't wait for the doctor to get in the room and set my mom straight. Zippy wasn't a hallucination, my tumor was shrinking, and I'd be cancer free within a year.

A knock at the door, and Dr. Weiss came in.

"Hey you two," he said with a smile. This could be reassuring. Then again, do doctors ever not smile when they say hello?

"So," I chimed up, "let's cut to the chase. Please, tell my mom that my tumor has shrunk so she can take a breather."

Dr. Weiss closed the door and looked into his file while he regained composure. He scratched his head and put the x-ray from the CT scan on the lit whiteboard. "Gabe, I wish I could tell your mom that."

My guts sank and I felt as though I'd slammed into a brick wall. My mom scanned Dr. Weiss' face for explanation and asked, "What do you mean by that?"

"Mrs. Perkins, Gabe's tumor hasn't shrunk. If anything it's continuing to grow."

My mom slapped her hand over her mouth as if something horrible was going to fall out. She looked at me and then she allowed it to fall out, "I knew it."

Stunned I just sat there staring from the floor to my mom and back to Dr. Weiss. "But I've been doing chemo for months. Hasn't that helped? With anything? I mean you have to be joking." I waited. "Please tell me you're joking."

"Something as serious as this wouldn't be much of a joking matter," said the doctor.

Staring at the tile floor, I asked, "What can I do?"

"At this point, with how large the tumor is and its placement, along with the fact that we've already tried the chemo, there's nothing much that we really could do."

"Dr. Weiss, there must be something, surgery? Anything?" asked my mom.

Dr. Weiss took his glasses off, and wiped his face either as if he'd let a tear fall, or he was exasperated. "Sheila, the surgery would be a waste of money. Not only a waste of money but too dangerous. The odds of him living through the impact of having such a large mass removed from his brain would be slim to none."

"How long do we have?" asked my mom.

"Given the rapid growth, and the placement, I'd say at most two months."

"So what do I do now? Just wait to die?"

"I'm not sure I would put it that way, Gabe," said Dr. Weiss, "I would say that you live, live the fullest life you can, while you can. I'm not a god. I can't predict if you will die or how long you will live. All I can say is that the prognosis doesn't look good."

My mom, still speechless just stared at the floor as if maybe it could help provoke something to say. As if the floor would open up and swallow her whole.

"Well, given that it's my only option, what's dying going to be like?" I asked Dr. Weiss. Right when I asked him I heard my mom heave for air.

The doctor put his pen to his lips and looked me square in the eye, "I haven't got the slightest clue. Everyone passes in different ways. Different emotional struggles, different physical struggles. Everyone has their own path. Each path has its own walker and each walker his own path. However, I do believe that it's less important how you die, but how much you live up until the point that you do. You've gained knowledge today about your path that not everyone has the opportunity to know."

"I already knew I had cancer what's a time limit going to do about it?"

"It's allowing you to fully appreciate what time you have."

"Are you trying to say that it's a good thing that I know I could die soon?"

"No, I'm simply saying that you know how close death is to you. Not everyone does. Look at the benefit of the hand dealt to you, rather than the negativity it brings."

●

The car ride home was solemn. It was more as if someone had already died rather than being given the death sentence. In that moment there I realized I couldn't live as if I was dying. I had to live with purpose, because any breath inhaled could be the last from this beautiful world.

I shook the silence in the car, "I've decided something, mom."

"And what's that?"

"I don't want to live as if I'm dying. I want to live and breathe offering my life to the world, giving everything that's in me that's positive. It seems as though ever since the beginning of the school year when I found out that I had this mess, that all I could think of was my dying. I don't want to live as though I am through."

"I would like that."

"I would like for you to treat me as if I'm here. Not on my death bed. Treat me as your son and as if you never heard the words fall from the doctors lips that all the chemo done was in vain. There are two decisions as to how my last few steps of my path could be walked. Rather than living them in a cloud of negativity it needs to be walked spreading love and that's really all I can give."

"I find it so strange," said my mom as she kept her eyes on the road, "that being boy your age, and going through what life has dealt you, that you can still have your head on straighter than mine." She looked over at me and let a smile out.

When we got home she made us an early dinner. "Not much in the fridge," She said leaning over as she grabbed overly processed deli meat out of a refrigerator door. "How about some fried bologna sandwiches?"

"My favorite sounds good to me." To anyone else, these sandwiches may raise the same emotion of the likes of canned meat, which probably isn't a very fond one. They probably cost only ten cents per sandwich but I grew up with these. Ever since I was a kid whenever my mom would whip one of these up I would let out a little squeal in one of the deep corners of my mind.

There's just something about the way the processed deli meat hits the frying pan. That pan sprayed heavy with canola in a can. The way the white bread is buttered and thrown on the pan along with the grease of the bologna. It's the way mom puts a piece of equally as processed American cheese in the middle of the two bologna pieces that makes it all come together. Something in the way when you bite into it you knew you were home.

Ding-a-dong. The doorbell rang and I was brought down from my nostalgic cloud nine.

My mom was still in the process of making the sandwiches so she just shouted, "Come on in."

The door slung open and Darla pranced in, "Mmmm something smells delicious!" she said as she ran up and hugged me from behind.

Mom turned around and looked at me with wide eyes and I slightly shook my head hoping she'd get that I didn't want to tell Darla just yet.

"Man, you guys look glum. I don't know why, with all this wonderful cooking," she said as she plopped down in the seat next to me.

I looked right at her and lied, "I just wasn't expecting you was all. You flew in like a tornado, girl."

"How about a bologna sandwich?" my mom offered. "It's not much, but I have a tendency for liking them."

"That would be wonderful."

"So, tell me how was school," I asked her, trying to keep her interest because I didn't want to have to tell her what I found out today. Just a few more minutes of her seeing me with a possible future is all I wanted.

"It was wonderful," she started, and trailed off into her day.

We finished eating and my mom washed and put away our plates. "I'm gonna head out. My shift starts in a little while and I don't want to be late. Darla, stay as long as you like. Keep my little buddy company."

"Thanks Mrs. Perkins. Especially for the food, it was yummy," she said as she licked the mayo off of her fingers.

"Call me Sheila, hon."

When she left, right as the door was closing, Darla flipped her gaze from my mom to my face and fell serious, "What's going on, Gabe?"

"I need to talk to you about something." I told her as I led her by the hand from the table to the living room couch. They weren't far from one another but it was a necessary transition. The couch was much more comfy and I deemed it a suitable destination for breaking the news.

After I sat down I guided her to sit down right beside me. I turned my gaze from her hand to her beautiful green eyes. The middles burned orange in the shape of a sunflower. "Darla, I went to the doctor today."

She could almost read my face. As if I had it plastered on my forehead that I didn't have much time. She fought back tears and asked, "Oh, really? What happened?" as if she didn't already know.

"Chemo isn't helping the tumor."

"Oh," she said, fighting back tears.

"In fact, the tumor is growing."

"Oh," she said as the tears flowed past her eyelids. I reached up and wiped them away.

"They can't do surgery and there's nothing else that they can do to help. My doctor basically just told me it's out of their hands." I stared at her, and hesitated for a moment before continuing, "Darla, they told me I only have…"

She cut me off hysterically, "Don't say it. Please don't say anything else." She threw herself in my arms and rocked her body as she whispered, "I know Gabe. Please don't say another word, I don't want to have to hear it. I just want to hold you while I can."

"I'm not going anywhere today."

She peeled back from me and stared in my eyes and said, "I know." She kissed me heavily, "you know I love you, right?"

"Hopefully it's not just given the circumstances."

"Of course it's not. You have made me realize so much in these past few months." She itched her wrist, "You've made me realize how important it is to express anything meaningful to anyone. If anything, I hate that it's under these circumstances that I've told you how much I care for you."

"I do too."

"Doctors aren't always right you know?"

"You know, Darla." I said as I inhaled a whiff of her cocoa butter, "It would be understandable if you want to just break things off. Just leave them where they are and walk away. It wouldn't hurt my feelings if you did because I know you would be hurt worse in the end."

She looked at me with disgust. For a moment I even wondered if she was going to hit me but that's the furthest from what she did. She pulled me into her arms and cried, heaving so hard it felt like an earthquake. I pulled back from her and wiped the tears from her eyes. I kissed her pouty lips and she kissed mine back.

●

I was sitting in my room thinking back on the past couple months, I was hit with the epiphany that cancer had given me the best months of my life. Many people would say to a fifteen year old that they have their whole life ahead of them and that high school doesn't matter much. That it's just a fragment of time. That once you've gone off to college, began your career and started your family that you rarely even think of things that happened in high school. Most people would say that no teenager should worry about high school problems because they become a ripple in the pond of the past, just a shaded memory.

For me on the other hand, or any other kid my age having to deal with death by cancer or any other terminal illness, high school is what we have. That moment, in that place in time, is all that I had going for me. Some day when everyone grows up, moves off to college, begins their career, and starts their family, they'll forget their high school years because they're focused more on the present.

After I die, I will have nothing to hold a light to other than these childhood years. I'll most likely die before this year ends and though people may grieve for the loss of the misfit boy they barely knew, they eventually will grow and change with their constant moving lives, while I remain in the shadows of high school's past.

I'll never grow old. I'll never know what it feels like to have grandchildren or children for that matter. I'll never have to worry about paying the mortgage on time. I'll never be able to have the dreaded feeling of finding a wrinkle etched across my forehead. A wrinkle, being the telltale sign of aging, as a ring is to a tree. Something that most people try to erase with surgery is something that I would love to be able to experience. Wrinkles across one's skin aren't something horrible one should want to hide, it lets people know what kind of a life you've led. I love the idea of forehead, mouth, and eye wrinkles. If you have them on your forehead you've probably had a life full of surprise. As for the crow's feet and marionette lines, they show the world how much you've smiled.

Forever I'll remain in Neverland as the same young boy I always was.

I sat on the edge of the overlook. The same spot where I've been coming for years since the death of my father, and the same spot where I've been coming since I found out I had cancer. The same exact spot where I would hope I would find Zippy.

I saw her sitting there on the ledge, long golden blonde wavy hair floating in the wind.

"You came looking for me," said Zippy.

"I did," I told her, as I stood. I didn't bother sitting down today. I looked out at the open valley. "I'm sure you know why."

"I do. Just because you can't always see me doesn't mean that I'm not around."

"I've figured. How long have you known."

"About what?"

I looked at her doubting her naivety, then back out at the open space, "About the fact that I was going to die from cancer."

"Some time now."

"So, you came to bring hope in my life while knowing it would still be ripped away in the end? That's just wonderful. Why would God even send me a guardian angel if there was nothing she could guard me from?"

"You believe there's a God now?"

"I do."

She put her hand on my arm and said, "That's exactly why he would send me to you, Gabe."

"I'm not quite sure I understand what you mean."

"Think of it like this. God has a plan for everyone and knows what the path of someone's life before they even live it. Sometimes people veer off of the path that he has laid before them and it's up to that person to get back on the path. He'll try and guide you back onto it, but people have human will and where there's a will, there's a way. He's not going to force anyone back on the path but he surely will nudge."

"Are you trying to say you came here to get me back on the path of cancer?" I looked at her and squinted my eyes, "Zip, I don't think that makes you a guardian angel I think that would make you the angel of death."

"Again with this angel of death thing," She said as she pulled her hand off of my arm, "Honestly, if an angel of death took you off to a place of fluffy clouds, would it really be such a bad thing? Anyways, no, that's not what I meant at all. He loves you, Gabe. He knew what your life would entail. He knew that you were going to fight a big battle. However, it was you who strayed off of the path of your love for him, regardless as to whether or not it was your fault. He kept loving you, and he knew when you were about to deal with something that no one should go through alone. He knew that you were going to need him. That's why he sent me. Because even though you're dying from cancer on Earth, you don't have to die eternally. I'm just here to guard you away from the thoughts and emotional damage that it can cause."

"That sounds cool and all but you do realize that I've only been seeing you since I've had cancer. That I've been seeing you more often as the tumor has been growing."

"I know what you're getting at, Gabe. It would be much easier to believe that I am just a hallucination caused by the cancer, wouldn't it?"

I nodded without looking at her face.

"But then on the other hand, I don't think you would've sought me out today had you actually believed that. Why waste your time if I'm just some hallucination?"

"Because I've grown use to you?" I told her, but deep down I knew she was right. I knew I believed that she was an angel.

"You don't believe that. I know you don't. I almost feel sympathetic towards you. It would be much easier to believe that I was a hallucination, wouldn't it?"

I stared at here for a few minutes and then looked down at my feet and nodded. By the time I looked back at her to open my mouth and say something she had already disappeared.

●

As I headed back toward the house the sky had started to darken. There were various shades of blue. From the treetops the sky was painted a pale yellow/blue, the further up I looked there was a mixing of red and pinks until the purplish sky met with a deep dark blue. I could see the stars begin to peek out from under the daytime sky. I've always had a likeness for stars, but never realized what it was that interested me the most in them. What it was about them, I wasn't sure.

Until that very moment.

Stars. Trillions of stars in the sky. Stars held within a galaxy, within an ever expanding universe.

Giant exploding balls of gas. By the time we see a star it's already exploded hundreds of years ago. Tiny little planets, somewhere so far off that we just now have the opportunity to see its beautiful life catch fire in the sky.

I now imagine my life as a star. One could only hope that somewhere, hundreds of years away, after the soul has left the body that someone will still see that explosion of life. To leave one's mark on the world in such a cataclysmic way that will leave an imprint on everyone who sees it.

I never really had a reason to sit down and think about why I was so infatuated with a star. Being put into a position of having to evaluate death makes you wonder what kind of a legacy you may leave behind. Sometimes you lead a life to simply impact another's. Though you may never know your purpose in the world, somehow or another you are a miniscule piece of an elaborate puzzle.

# Chapter 8

After having slept half of the day away I went to check the mail. Right when I opened the door I saw Tony sitting on the front porch, legs sprawled out as his back leaned against the paneling of the house. I hadn't seen him in a while, since my last chemo appointment. It had been nearly a week.

"Long time no see, asshole," said Tony.

"That's a great way to greet someone you haven't even bothered to call."

"At least I have the decency to come over after having to hear the whole school talking about how my best friend found out his chemo wasn't doing crap for his tumor and he had been given a short leash on what's left of his life."

"I've been dealing with things, Tony."

"A week, dude. Seriously? You can't even tell me anything?"

"Look, between getting things straight in my head, and getting things straight with my mom I didn't have time…"

"You didn't have time to tell me, but you had time to tell Darla."

"Why are you just sitting out here? You could've rang the doorbell so I could let you in.

You know instead of just sitting out here like a creep."

"Well, you could've told me chemo wasn't working instead of me having to hear it from the whole school."

I sat down next to him on the stoop, "I'm sorry."

"That's bull, man. You know it is."

"I haven't even seen you in a week?"

"Pick up the phone?"

"Well you know now."

"Dude, I heard the rumors around school last week. Two whole days after you found out. I was so steamed that I found out from the kids at school. I didn't even want to believe it. So I waited around for you to come over or call me or something." He shook his head and sized me up, "But no you're way too wrapped up in yourself to give your best friend a heads up."

Tony looked around, stood up, and walked towards the door. Looking back he said, "Come on, I don't want to cause a scene out here. Plus I'm hungry."

"Good luck, there's probably hardly anything in there. Mom doesn't really have a grasp on grocery shopping. For her it's more like a milk and bread run."

"I'm good with some bread."

We went inside and I leaned against the wall as he searched through the kitchen for food. He stopped rummaging through the fridge and looked back at me. "What I'm not good with is being the last to know about my bud having cancer kick his butt in."

"You already knew it though. Maybe you weren't on my mind as being the first to tell."

Tony started laughing and walked over to the sink. He looked out the window and laughed psychotically as he used his hands to hold his weight against the counter. He flung himself toward me and finally shouted, "Are you out of your mind? I've been your best friend since you were five years old and your ass is going to tell me some mess about 'Oh maybe you weren't the first person I wanted to tell'? That's insane and you know it. I get that you're going through stuff, Gabe. Don't leave me out of your life though. You keep pushing people away and pushing people away. You have to stop it. It's freaking me out. Just be my old buddy again. Please?"

I looked at him and down at the floor. "I know, but it freaks me out too."

"You're my best friend!" He started crying and hyperventilating to the point where I thought he was going to pass out. I reached out and grabbed him in a shoulder hug. "I'm so freaking worried about you, like you're the only other person who's put up with my crap. You're the only one I've ever put myself on the line for."

"I'm not going anywhere. I know I should've at least called you to let you know but honestly I wasn't even ready to tell anybody."

"Ugh," he grunted as he wiped his face off and walked over to the couch, "Then riddle me this good fellow, why did everyone at school know?"

"Probably Darla. She came over the afternoon I found out. She was just stopping by, you know. It just happened to be that it was right after my doctor's appointment and my mom and I were eating and she joined us. I wasn't even really ready to tell her yet but she could feel the tension in the air. Just, you know that tension of having something you're trying extremely hard not to tell and they can feel it."

"Women, always having to run their mouths," he flicked on the T.V. and sprawled out along the couch.

"Don't say it like that," I said, defending Darla.

"So, if she didn't run her mouth then how did everyone know within a half a day at school?"

"My guess is she probably was so upset that she told one of her friends. Then the game of telephone played itself out and 'tada', everyone knows."

"Yeah," Tony said wiping his eyes with the back of his sleeve. "You're probably right. So how's that going? With Darla and all?"

"Perfect. I really couldn't have imagined it any better."

"That's good. At least if she's going to be a big mouth, she'll be good to you at the same time."

"It is pretty crappy that you had to find out through the rest of the high school before I got a chance to let you know."

"No shit."

"But then it doesn't make any sense to be pissed at someone you may not have around much longer, does it?" I asked with a hint of humor.

Tony looked at me and laughed, "Nah, man, I guess it really doesn't."

"I really don't want to even think about it anymore."

"What? The cancer?"

"I don't want to think about the fact that I probably will end up dying at some point in the near future. I'd like to just live it out doing good stuff, having the time of my life."

"Then do it. You at least somewhat know how long you have left. Me on the other hand, I could get hit by a car while crossing the road tomorrow."

"I could too."

●

Later that night I got a phone call from Darla, inviting me and mom over for dinner the next day. Why would anyone turn down a fun time at the Lively's house?

The name in itself is pretty ironic. At least from where I see things. A boy fighting a battle against cancer dating a girl named 'Lively'. Pretty ironic but maybe it just puts even more emphasis on the fact that we were supposed to be together, maybe not to have a future together but to go through this together, as friends, as a couple.

Mom and I arrived at the porch of the Lively's. Mom had a jug of tea and a baked 'homemade' custard which she probably just picked up in the bakery section of the grocery store and put into a plastic container. It was somewhat of an offering. Not just for inviting us over for dinner but an offering of thanks to the family that helped so much with the medical bills my mom would've taken on had it not been for their hospitality.

Darla greeted us at the door wearing a button down shirt with cherries printed on it, and a red pencil skirt. "Gabe!" She shouted, as her face lit up. She hugged me by the neck with such intensity that it felt as though my head might pop off. Finally she let go and took me by the hand, "Come inside you two. Mom's made a feast for y'all."

We went inside and my mom took the custard into the kitchen while I handed my coat off to Darla for her to put up. When she was done hanging up my coat in the hall closet she took my hand once again and led me to the dining room.

"Do you think they need help bringing anything in from the kitchen?" I asked Darla.

"Nope, I think they have it all under control. Mom already started setting out some of the food on the table. All we really need is drinks and the chicken but I think they've got that all covered."

"Good," I said, I wasn't really mad at her or anything about telling everyone at school. It wasn't her fault that I hadn't told Tony yet.

There was a long oak table in the middle of the dining room that was decorated with salads and side dishes in glass containers. Along the walls there were shelves that held delicate china and wine glasses. There was a large wine rack that held what looked to be hundreds of bottles. Her parents must have been collecting them for ages.

We stood against the red wall of the dining room, "You're not mad at me are you?" she looked at me and then across the room, "You know, for talking to people about it? I heard Tony was a little ticked off when he found out. I'm sure you were mad when you realized I had told someone."

I looked at her and couldn't be mad at her even if I really wanted to, "No. There was enough time for me to have told Tony. It would be silly wasting time being mad at you. I know that you probably were just so overwhelmed and upset yourself that you needed someone to talk to and reached out to one of your friends."

"Yeah. Why didn't you tell him sooner?"

"I just haven't been in the mood to talk about things much this past week."

"You haven't even talked to me hardly." She looked at the table, then back to me, "I know you've been dealing with stuff so I won't hold it against you."

241

Our parents came out of the kitchen. Mom carrying the sweet tea and Darla's dad bringing out the chicken.

Mr. Lively looked at everyone standing around the table, "We can sit, unless, of course everyone wants to eat like a giraffe tonight."

We all took up a seat and began passing dinner around the table. I stacked my plate full with different vegetables and carbs.

"So, what's the occasion for dinner tonight? Nothing really seems celebratory at this moment," I said.

Mr. Perkins perked up and said, "Of course there's something to celebrate tonight. Life. We all are alive and breathing in this very fleeting moment. And for now we all have something to celebrate and be happy about."

Everyone smiled and Mrs. Perkins joined in the conversation, "We actually invited you and you're mom to dinner because we would like to talk about the fair we are having for you." She hesitated for a moment and then continued, "We thought that given the news that has arisen in the past week we might should have the fair sooner, rather than later."

"I would like to enjoy my own fair, rather than it being a memorial service," I laughed but looked around and realized that I made the mood turn somewhat solemn. "I was only joking," I reassured everyone and they all forced a laugh.

As we ate I realized how fortunate I really was. Not only was I able to have an amazing mom and girlfriend but I was surrounded by people who actually care about my life. I knew I was loved I may be different than most or have a different path than many people but I knew that regardless of anything that may come my way, in that moment I was loved.

I zoned back into the conversation and joined in, "Mr. and Mrs. Perkins," I hesitated as they looked my way and nodded, "Mom and Darla, I just want to thank you all. Somewhat because of everything that you're doing for me financially and mentally but mostly because of the emotional help you're bringing to my life. In a time when I could really look at my life as a nightmare, I look at it as the best thing that's ever happened to me simply because I can truly see how beautiful a life I have, to have so many people around me who love me. And, well, I love each of you for that."

Small chatters of 'we love you too' came from around the table all at once. It was true though, everything I'd just said. I'm a million times more fortunate than someone who hasn't had to face this demon. People who live their life day to day without any battle popping up don't have the ability to see life for what it truly is, an opportunity to grow as a human being. Not just for the likes of growing as a person but growing spiritually and growing within yourself and really appreciating who you are, in the moment you have.

"So," I spoke up once again, "When were you guys thinking of moving the fair up to?"

"What are your plans like for this weekend?" asked Darla.

"I was planning on hanging out with you, but I guess we can just hang out there, eh?"

"Yeah, I'd like that."

"Alright then," said Mr. Lively, "Let's get down to business. We need to take down all of the flyers that are already around town and put up new ones. The old ones have a date on them for next month, and since we're moving it up to this weekend we need to do that as soon as possible."

"What about all the booths, and people working them?" I asked.

"We've already got that covered. When Darla told us about what the doctors told you, we went ahead and talked to the rental company to see if they would be available this upcoming weekend and they were able to move things around in their schedules so that they'd be available to help out."

I nibbled at a piece of bread and mumbled, "I can't believe how selfless everyone has been for me." I wasn't sure if I'd meant to say it out loud. It was more of a thought that had drifted past my lips.

Mr. Lively looked up at me. Underneath his chiseled features, his tan, his oversized glasses, and his button-down plaid shirt he had a soft spot for me. "You have to realize something, Gabe. This town hasn't seen too many other kids in your situation. It's not every day that a teenager is fighting a battle as tough as the one you're up against. If their thinking is anything in line with my thinking, they probably feel empathy towards a situation like yours." He wiped his mouth with a napkin. "They also must be pretty astonished. I for one am amazed at how you're handling everything that's been thrown your way. Not just how you're handling it, but also the way you're allowing it to change and affect you. You're changing from an adolescent boy into a man. It's really quite the extraordinary to see. I'm sure that people around town are pretty amazed with the fact that a fifteen year old could tackle on such a beast."

●

It was the morning of the fair. It was a few weeks since my last chemo treatment and I was already hungry to eat everything in sight. (Without the help of my buddy Tony.)

Crawling out of the bed I could smell my mom's cooking wafting through the house. It practically lifted me up off the bed. I threw my hoodie on over my T-shirt and pajama pants and floated down the small shadowed hall. Rounding the corner I saw my three favorite people in the world cooking in the kitchen.

"What's this all about?" I asked with a smile on my face.

Tony, Darla, and mom turned around and smiled back. They all gave their good mornings and waved me to come sit down at the table.

"Sure you guys don't need any help with anything?"

"We got it all under control," my mom said.

I was surprised that they had all came over that morning. They were already going to be doing so much at the fair but the fact that they were already up and at it before seven was beyond amazing. I really was surrounded by some phenomenal people.

I took a seat at the dining room table where a pitcher of orange juice was sitting and poured myself a glass.

"So," Darla said as she brought a plate of pancakes over, "I hope you slept well and brushed your teeth of course."

My mom turned around, "Trust me Darla, you don't want to know what his morning breath smells like."

"You can say that again," Tony said as he walked over with a bowl of fruit and a plate of bacon.

"Well, I'm sorry, but y'all are just going to have to deal with some morning breath for a half hour. Brushing my teeth would ruin the taste of the breakfast that my two best friends and mom took the time to make." I put pancakes and bacon on my plate, took a bite, and looked up cheekily at the three of them.

"Fine by me," said mom.

"So," jumped in Darla, "since it's getting chilly out we were able to rent some big tents to put the food carts in. We figured with it getting cool and everything outside, at least that will give people a place to sit, rest, and get warm."

"I like warm."

"You know, Gabe, I'm really happy that you were up for doing the fair this weekend. Thanks for going along with it."

"It's no problem. I should really be thanking you guys for figuring everything out so quickly."

"Alright," Tony said. "Start shoveling some food in your mouth. You, unlike the rest of us here, still have to get ready."

We all ate and chatted little small talk conversations about things that were going on in our lives. Of course everyone knew just about everything that was going on in my life. That's sort of what happens when you get a life threatening disease and you drop out of school, in a one horse town at least. Your life becomes an open book.

It was nice hearing everything that was going on with my two buddies though. Seems like ever since I found out about the big 'C', I had lost the will to ask what was going on with those around me. Tony finally had gotten his grades up. Not only had he gotten his grades up but he had gotten them up to B's and C's. Trust me, B's and C's for him are like an average kid getting on the honor roll and becoming valedictorian. It's a big deal.

Darla, of course, was doing great in school. She'd started taking up writing since she found out I had cancer. Apparently she had been writing away. She'd written poems like a mad woman and had been hiding them. One day her mom found her notebook filled with poems and encouraged her to do something with them. She's been competing in contests and just one second place in a state-wide contest. Surprisingly it was the first time she'd ever told me about it but then I never gave her much time to actually tell me about herself. The focus was always on me.

After breakfast mom and company cleared things away and rushed me off to get ready. I couldn't blame them. We'd talked and ate for a good hour and we only had two hours for me to get ready and get to the fair. I hopped in the shower and there was a knock on the door.

"Dear God," I mumbled to myself, "I hope that's not Darla." I answered the knock, "Still showering."

The door opened and my heart thumped.

"Don't worry cancer boy." It was just Tony, "It's just me. Your mom asked me to bring this outfit in here for you. You'll look good in it. Kinda fancy but you'll look good in it."

I poked my head out of the shower curtain to look at the outfit, "Dang, it is a nice suit. I'm not one for suits but it's nice."

"Your mom said she picked it up yesterday for you. Wasn't sure whether or not you'd fit it but had hoped it would."

I returned to showering, "Where did she get the money to buy me a suit?"

"Not sure, not my business. My guess is that she's your mom and she loves the hell out of you for some reason. She probably stuck any leftover pocket change or money going unused in a jar for you so she could get it for you."

"Yeah, probably."

I finished showering and hoped out. My hair had barely started growing back, but it was really just patchy peach fuzz. Fortunately for me my mom had also bought me a nice hat. Not like a top hat or anything just a cool fedora. Fedoras are cool by the way.

I strutted my stuff down the hall into the living room.

"Meeee-ow!" Darla said from the kitchen. She had curled her hair and was wearing a burnt orange cocktail dress with brown stockings.

Mom was sitting on the sofa wearing a pair of khaki pants and a gold button down shirt. Tony was missing.

"Where's Tony?"

"Here I am."

I turned around and coming down the hall from my mom's room was Tony, wearing a suit that matched mine.

"Oh, my gosh, is that how I look?"

"You guys look great," said Darla.

"I thought the two partners in crime should match."

My mom grabbed the camera from the coffee table, "Why don't you guys all huddle in for a photo."

Once we got to the fair Tony, Darla, and I hopped out of the car.

"You're not coming with us?"

"I have to run to the diner to pick up a few more things."

We had a huge food venue area and mom's diner had its own booth. The people running the game booths were donating their time, as were the people running the food booths. Time, as well as money was being donated.

Once mom had driven off, my two musketeers and I took it upon ourselves to head off through the fair and see what all was going on. There weren't too many people there yet and most of the booths were still setting up and workers were prepping them but you could still get a vibe that everyone was happy to be there.

There were carnival games and rides of all kinds. People from all over town had pitched in where they could. As you entered from the parking lot there was a red ticket booth and a gate. Past the gate there was a long pathway lined with game booths and rides. All booths were lit up with strands of flashing lights. At the end of the row of games were a large stage and a ferries wheel off to the right. It would really be amazing to see when the sun went down. It felt overwhelming to see so many people pitching in their hand to help a kid they didn't even know.

"You guys! I get my own ferris wheel!"

Darla laughed and wrapped her arm around me.

"You know, Darla," said Tony, "I'm really glad that you and Gabe are together."

"Oh, yeah? You're not jealous that I steal time away from you and your buddy?"

"No, it's pretty cool that my best friend has been having some of the best days of his life and it may sound stupid but you being there with him through all this really does make this some of the best days of his life."

"Thanks, Tony." Darla twisted her eyebrows, confused at his kindness.

We continued walking down the row of games and didn't even say much to one another as we walked around but just having each other there, in that moment we felt that the silence meant more to us than anything we could say. In that moment we were forever, and in that moment we were young and free.

We saw Tony's dad working at the ferris wheel. "Hey guys, I'm going to see if he needs some help with anything. I'll catch up with you guys in a while," Tony said.

"Sounds like a plan, Stan," I said and we did a fist bump.

"Really," Darla said with a smirk, "fist bump? Very cute."

"Don't hate," Tony said without turning around as he was walking towards his dad's Ferris wheel.

"We need to ride that at some point tonight, Gabe," she said.

I put my arm around her and agreed, "That we do."

We walked around the carnival a little bit more, her arms around my waist and my arm around her petite shoulders.

"Don't take this the wrong way," she began, "but, I'm almost glad that you got cancer."

She looked up into my eyes and a grin escaped across her face. For a second I had to wonder what the heck was wrong with this woman. "Huh?"

"Okay well, it's not that I like the fact that you're sick or anything. It just opened up my eyes to the fact that I've always had feelings for you, you know? It was like I was sitting in this room of denial and when I found out that you had cancer a major light was turned on."

"Like a light being shed on how much you liked me?"

"Not even just about me liking you but about the fact that life is so fleeting. We never know what's going to happen. It's almost better to live freely with a sense of carefulness, rather than being worried about day to day issues. It's better to focus on now and what's actually happening because you never know what tomorrow may hold, if it even holds anything."

"You're pretty dreamy, Darla," I said as I twisted a lock of her hair.

Just then we heard a voice call out, "There you two are." It was Darla's dad. He was wearing black pants, a white button down, and a pair of red suspenders and a red bowtie.

"Whoa, Mr. Lively. You look like a mime."

"Hm," he said as he popped his suspenders, "Well, I guess you'd be right. Fancy, eh?"

"Yeah, definitely fancy," I said as Darla chuckled.

"Gabe, your mom just got back from the diner. Said she could use a little help getting stuff out of the car. You wouldn't mind if I stole my little girl here to help me run around a bit?"

"No, not a problem."

Darla waved and walked off with her dad. I watched them walk for a good minute before I decided I should probably be going to help my mom.

I jogged my way over to my mom's car and helped her get the food out.People were beginning to fill in the parking lot.

"'Bout time, you came over, crazy boy." She lifted a box from the back of her car, "I was almost wondering if Darla's dad hadn't relayed the message."

"No I'm just slow sometimes."

"Alright, well let's go ahead and take this stuff to the booth."

I grabbed another box and we took the food up to the covered venue and helped her staff get things ready.

"It looked like people were starting to pile in, didn't it?" I asked mom.

"I thought the same thing too but I was hoping I would have a little bit more time to get things settled and ready."

"You're just excited is all, mom, things are looking great."

"You think?"

"Yeah, I wouldn't worry about it too much. I mean, have you looked around at how amazing everything is?"

She let out a sigh, brushed a hair back off of her face, and leaned in towards me, "I guess you're right." She kissed me on the head and continued unpacking her boxes.

After about an hour of helping her finish setting up she asked, "Why don't you go on out there and enjoy the fair?

"Are you sure you don't need any more help?"

"You've done enough, go have fun."

I pulled back the thick canvas siding of the tent and stepped outside.

"Psst," I heard someone say.

At first I thought it may have been Darla trying to get my attention. I turned around and there was no one there. I went around the tent and still didn't see anyone.

"Psst," I heard it again.

I turned around and it sounded like it was coming from the nearby woods. I looked around at the fair behind me and no one was watching me. I walked into the woods and felt a tap on my shoulder and turned around.

There in front of me stood Zippy. She wore her hair long, with a chain of braids and multicolored wildflowers wove around the crown of her head. Her cream colored dress drifted in the breeze and draped around her ankles with flecks of gold shimmering around its edges. Today she really looked like an angel.

"Hello stranger," she said as her eyes sparkled.

"Hey, you. Where have you been?"

"Oh, around."

"I see. Well why were you calling me out to the woods?"

"Because it would be a little bit strange for everyone at the fair to see a boy who has cancer talking to thin air. Don't you think?"

"I have to give it to you, you're one pretty smart angel. So what's up?" I looked at her dress and realized she could have only been dressed up for one occasion alone. "Oh, I see. Is it time? I really didn't think I had much time left but I didn't think I'd end up going today."

She let out a guttural laugh, "Don't be silly. I just wanted to say hello on your big day."

"I'm not sure that I'd say this is necessarily my big day."

"The whole town is here just for you, Gabe. I would say that it is." She looked at me for a moment and continued, "I noticed that things are going great with you and Darla."

"They really are, Zip."

"Well, I'm glad. I just wanted to pop in and say 'hello' to the guest of honor. I don't want to keep your friends and family waiting."

I didn't want to keep my friends and family waiting either but it was almost difficult to leave Zippy all alone in the woods.

"Right, so I'll see you around?"

She shook her head, "You don't need me anymore."

I shook my head in disagreement, "Of course I do."

"You're right where you need to be."

I gave her a smile and waved goodbye.

On the way back through the carnival I snagged a corn dog for me and a corn dog for Darla. I found her helping at her mom's cotton candy booth. I waited in the long line to get to her.

"Thought you might get tired of the sugar," I said as I pointed the corn dog at her.

"Your thoughts were right!" she replied.

"Darla, why don't you go play some games with Gabe?"

"I thought you'd never ask," she said as she kissed her mom on the cheek.

"Thanks, Mrs. Lively."

Darla jumped out from behind the cotton candy booth and led me by the hand on a race through the fair.

"Remember what I said I really wanted to do before the fair was over?" Darla asked.

"The Ferris wheel, right?"

"Exactly," she said with excitement.

"Wait, though," I said gripping on her hand tightly so she'd stop running. "It's hardly even dusk, why don't we wait until later when it's dark, so we can sit under the stars together?"

"You're pretty romantic, Gabe." She said and she leaned in and pecked me on the cheek. "Sure, why not."

For the next hour or two we walked around and played the carnival games. We won a few stuffed animals along the way, little trophies of love. After an hour or so of playing games I heard the band playing.

Darla turned to me and shouted, "Do you hear that!?"

"The music?" I asked.

"Yeah let's go watch!" she said and off we were on another run through the carnival.

We got to the edge of the crowd hanging around the bandstand and worked our way to center stage. It wasn't any well-known band or anything, just a local band, but it was still a band. For a local band they weren't that bad. Of course they played mostly covers of songs that had been made well known by famous bands but they did the songs justice. If you closed your eyes for a split second you could almost imagine that you were at a real concert.

After the music was played and the band was finished with their set list Darla's parents and my mom got on stage.

"Thank youuuu, Rural Hall." My mom laughed, as she covered the phone and whispered to Darla's dad, "I always wanted to say that." She took her hand off of the microphone, "Well folks, I just wanted to say how thankful I am that all of you made it out today. I see a lot of familiar faces but for those I don't know, I'm Sheila Perkins, Gabe Perkins' mom. It means the world to us that you took the time out of your day to come and take part in this celebration of life. I also would really like to thank Mr. and Mrs. Lively for being such a huge part of the fair. Without them, it wouldn't have been nearly as fantastic. I'd like to go ahead and hand the mic over to Mr. Lively. He has a few announcements to make."

Mom handed the microphone over to Darla's dad, "Thank you Sheila. We consider it a blessing that we have had the ability to help you and your son out during this trying time. We also would like to thank all of you," he said as he motioned towards the audience, "for making it out. Especially to those of you who helped run a booth or donated your time and money in any way for this event to take place. With it being the closing of the night, we'd like to go ahead and announce the profits that were made this evening, and how much money will be placed in the Gabe Perkins Fund." Mrs. Lively handed the envelope to Mr. Lively, and he opened the envelope and pulled out a card.

"Wow." He said surprised, "Get ready you guys, because this deserves a drum roll. You were all very generous."

The drum roll began. Mr. Lively continued, "Tonight's fair in conjunction to the money collected at the grocery stores around local towns raised," he took a pause, "Forty Two Thousand Dollars."

I felt my jaw drop as the crowd roared. I looked at Darla.

"Darla."

"I know," she said back.

I realized in that moment that all that money shouldn't have been wasted on me especially given the fact that a lot of the medical bills had already been paid by Darla and Jake's parents.

Darla looked up at me, "Do you think we could still ride the ferris wheel?"

"Of course we can."

We walked over to the ferris wheel and Tony greeted us at the ride. "You two be safe. Too much movement and this thing could topple over." He winked at us and walked back to the control board.

"No worries," I said as we put the bar over our lap.

As we rode to the top I could feel the crisp air biting at my fingers. I looked over at Darla and could tell that it was nipping at hers too. "Let me hold your hands. You must be cold."

"You read me like a book," she said as she bundled up close to me. "You know, Gabe," she said as she glanced out over the stars in space, "No matter what happens I'll always love you," she looked back into my eyes and we kissed long and hard. We continued to kissed, her lips pressing against mine, almost forgetting that the world was passing us by for a good ten minutes.

I pulled away from her, still stuck in a trance by her sunflower etched, green eyes.

After realizing how long we'd been up there I looked over the side and saw Tony just staring at us. "Thought I'd give y'all some privacy up there," he shouted.

"I guess this was as private as we could be with you watching, eh?"

"Guess you're right."

Tony began pressing buttons and we slowly made our way down.

# Chapter 9

Christmas passed along with New Years but the whole time I couldn't help but think about how much money was raised at the fair. It was all that I could do to keep my mind off of it. My mind wasn't even going to a place of greed or what I could do with the money, but rather how unfair it would be for me to keep all of that money. Not just of how unfair it would be for all the money to be used on me, but what would happen to all of the money that was going to be left over. I decided that I needed to have a talk with my mom.

One night she and I had sat down on the couch after dinner. I hadn't had much of an appetite lately, and when I was hungry I was usually too tired to even crawl out of bed to eat anything.

"Mom, I need to talk to you about something," I said as she turned her face from the T.V. towards me.

"What about?" she asked.

"It's about the funds that were raised at the fair. It just seems like there was a lot of outpouring from people, but I just don't see how we could possibly use it all on my medical bills. Like, I'm sure that I've caused a need for more money than you make at the diner but the Lively's were already helping out with the bills before the fair, you know?"

"I know. I've been thinking about the same thing since the fair. Honestly, we didn't think that people would be so selfless. We didn't even expect that many people to show up but they did." She hesitated and continued, "You know, Gabe, there are other costs that we may," she looked at her hands and back at me, "that I may incur. I wasn't really anticipating having to talk to you about this, but it's probably best that I talk to you about it rather than not."

"What kind of costs?"

"Gabe, you know where you stand with your illness. Dr. Weiss doesn't see you getting much better, in fact the tumor and you're side effects from the tumor are only getting worse."

"But maybe they're not?"

"You're beginning to lose your appetite that you finally got back from stopping chemo and you're always tired. Those aren't good things and Dr. Weiss has told you that those are symptoms from your body losing the fight."

"So what exactly are you getting at?"

"Gabe," she said as she rubbed the peach fuzz along my scalp, "At some point, possibly in the near future, it won't be just medical bills that I'll have to worry about. Funerals cost money too."

Dr. Weiss had told me that the sleepiness and loss of appetite were symptoms from it getting worse, but it never sank that it really was until just now. It took my mom facing me with what she was going to deal with after I was gone for me to see the reality of it all. I was going to die.

Tears running down my face, I asked my mom, "If any money is left over after the," I hesitated finding the right words, "'costs', can you do me a huge favor?

"Of course, what is it?"

"Keep that money as a fund to help another struggling family with a kid like me?"

My mom's eyes turned to gushing geysers as she grabbed me and held me close, "Of course, Gabe." She pulled back and wiped her tears off of her face onto the back of her sleeve. She looked me in the eyes, "I love what a selfless human being you've become. There aren't many like you in the world and it's a horrible thought that another addition to the group may be gone before his time."

I thought about what she just said and had an epiphany, "Mom, I'm not being cut short on my life and I'm definitely not going before my time."

She stared at me clueless.

"Think of it like this," I told her, "God has a plan for everyone, right?"

She nodded and I continued, "God had a path set out for me. He knew that there was a battle that I was going to face. I may have veered off of the path with God for a while, but I've been able to get back on it. You know, he let this battle happen, not because he's careless, but because he knew that something good would come out of it."

My mom nodded.

"Even if I die young, my life and soul for that matter has grown tremendously through this fight. People around us have given so much and not just for me, but for love. The love for someone they never knew and would probably never see again. That kind of generosity doesn't just happen coincidentally. It's an act of a higher being. There will be money left over from the fair's fund after I'm gone and that money will be able to help with some other family. My problem will have helped someone else."

She was speechless, so I returned myself to the conversation, "It's not just about the money either, mom. The people who came out and donated their time to help with the fair, the people who came to even spend money playing games, they were impacted as well. Doing something good for someone fills a void within the heart that often times we don't even realize is empty. Reaching out and helping someone else in need can heal some of the deepest aching that's rooted inside of us. Many people have been impacted by my cancer other than just myself. It's helped many people and will possible help many people in the future. I can't sit by and deny the fact that the cancer alone wasn't a blessing in disguise. I haven't been given a terminal illness. I've been given a terminal blessing."

●

It had been two days of miserable lying in bed. I didn't have the energy to get up and do anything, even if that anything meant going and taking in the atmosphere of the overlook. That would've been impossible given I could barely even walk to the bathroom.

On top of feeling like a sleep deprived zombie, I'd been puking off and on and been miserable of headaches. Mom was pulling double shifts at the diner since one of her assistant managers quit recently. We thought I may've caught a cold since it was January and bugs were going around like crazy. She kept a puke bucket at my bedside just in case.

Later in the night she brought home some fast food. Right when she walked through the door I vomited. This time I actually made the puke bucket. A couple days before when I began vomiting there were chunks of food in it, but lately it's been either dry-heaves or stomach bile. For the first time in the past two days I puked up blood.

"Mom," I said groggily.

She rushed in the room with a wet rag. I motioned her to look in the bucket. She glanced down and looked at me with a grimace.

"Gabe, this isn't good." She wiped the bile from the corner of my mouth, "I think we need to go to the E.R."

I nodded and she carried my featherweight body to the car. On the car ride to the hospital my mom called Dr. Weiss' cell phone. She was set on the fact that it wasn't just a cold, but that the cancer may be taking a turn for the worst. Calling Dr. Weiss may have ensured that by the time we got to the hospital he'd be there as well and open himself up for us.

We got to the emergency room and checked in. My mom talked to one of the hospital staff sitting behind the glass window.

"He needs to be taken back, now."

"It's going to be a while, ma'am. Everyone's sick. It's January, look around."

"You must be kidding me. He has cancer. e doesn't just have a cold. Look at him."

"Rest assured ma'am, he'll be fine," the woman said as she barely lifted her eyes off of the paperwork in front of her.

"Are you insane? Would you at least look at him and then at someone else in the room and tell me their situations are comparable."

"If you can't calm down I'm going to have to ask security to escort you from the waiting area."

"Are you insane?" my mom shouted at the woman.

"Security!"

Right as a security guard began walking over to my mom Dr. Weiss came walking through the doors. He ran over to my mom.

"What is going on here?"

"This woman," my mom pointed at the nurse, "is trying to call security on me while telling me that Gabe's situation is no different than anyone else in this waiting room."

"Where is he?"

She motioned her hand towards me.

He looked over at me and a solemn veil passed over his face. He looked at the nurse, "Did you even bother to look at him or ask his medical history?"

"Of course but it is the middle of January, so what's the rush?"

Dr. Weiss walked into the office where the woman was sitting and stood over her, "Are you out of your mind? He has a brain tumor and he was puking up blood and having issues staying awake with insane headaches and you're just going to let him sit there?!" Right when the nurse looked like she was going to open her mouth to respond he cut her off, "You're quite the idiot. How did you pass your nursing examination? If a boy came in here with a bullet wound in his head, gushing blood would you make him sit in the lobby?"

"Well, no," the nurse finally had the chance to say.

"Well consider him, to have a bullet wound to the head." The lady stared at him and he continued, "You've just proven how ignorant a nurse you really are. I'll deal with you later, but now I need a bed for him and vitals ran. I assume you're capable of doing that, correct?" She nodded and he continued, "Good then because you obviously aren't capable of telling high risk patients from ones who have the flu."

The nurse took me and my mom back to a room that had about ten beds lined up and down the walls. She had me go to one and pushed the curtain around it. She checked my temperature and blood pressure and everything else that a nurse usually does. Then Dr. Weiss came in and told me he was going to order an immediate CT Scan.

My mom and I waited in that cold, large room for two hours. While we waited the nurse hooked up an IV to my arm that was connected to two bags, one that had steroids, and one that had pain killers. The nurse brought me a can of ginger ale and crackers, hoping that one or the other may help with my stomach. I just sat there and eyeballed them, thinking in fear of the puking session that they may induce.

Finally we were taken up to have a CT Scan done. They took me up the elevator. I'd had quite a few CT Scan's done before especially since finding out I had cancer, but for some reason this one seemed more intense, was far more scarier. I looked at my mom and mouthed 'Thank You'. I'm not sure why, but at that moment it was everything that my heart could feel. It transcended the simplicity of her taking me to the hospital when I was sick or even for being so strong for me throughout the battle. She'd been my rock for my entire life.

After the scan my mom and I went downstairs again to wait in our little private corner of the large room with many beds. As we rounded the corner my eyes grew large, not because I felt overcome with the urge to vomit, but because of who I saw standing in front of me. Zippy. Right there as I sat on the bed I looked at her and back at my mom, then over to her again.

"You told me I wasn't going to see you again?" I said to her.

She put her finger to her lips in a gesture for me to stay quiet.

My mom stared at me, "Lay down, Gabe. You're starting to look sick again."

"I'm fine," I said as I shook my head. "It must be the pain killers," I laid back in my bed.

Usually I was beyond thrilled to see Zippy. It was the first time she'd actually been in the same room with me and my mom (or me and anyone else, for that matter). She walked by my mom once in passing, but never sat in the same room.

About an hour later Dr. Weiss came in the room. He took a moment to himself before putting the X-Ray on the light board. Just before turning the light on he rubbed his forehead with his hand. For a moment I wanted to think it was because it was the middle of the night, but deep down I knew that it was because he was about to have to tell me and my mom something horrible.

He turned the light on and I saw instantly why I'd been feeling so miserable lately. The tumor had grown tremendously since the last time I'd seen him. I knew things weren't going to go over so well, that things weren't turning in my favor. My mom didn't even seem surprised. She was seeing what she already had imagined was happening. I'm sure her thoughts were well in line with mine. None of us shed a tear. It was almost as though we'd already known since we arrived at the hospital that this wasn't going to be a sweet little visit.

Dr. Weiss pulled up a chair and sat down with his elbow resting on his knee and his chin resting in his palms. "I think it goes without saying that you're tumor has substantially grown. I wish it wasn't the case, but it looks as though it's forty percent larger than the last time we did a scan."

"How could it have grown so large, so quickly?" asked mom.

"I'm not sure," he took his glasses off and put them in his pocket. "Sometimes these things just happen, Sheila."

"Where do we go from here? What steps do we need to take?"

"I would recommend that he stays here from now on. Here or in hospice care."

"I don't want to go to hospice. That's where people go to die." I said without thinking of the emotional repercussions that would ensue.

"Then you stay here," said Dr. Weiss, "I'll make sure that you have nurses around you that are more equip to work with you. You'll have your own room and everything. That's my promise."

"How long do you think I have, Dr. Weiss?" I asked. I was scared as hell of what his answer might be, but I wanted to know. "From someone's viewpoint who has seen this sort of thing before."

"Gabe," he started, "everyone is very different. You are a strong boy, however given the circumstances of how your body's been acting, and what I've seen in other patients. I would say just enjoy the time you have, rather than worrying over how much time you have. Remind those around you of your love for them."

I nodded.

"You've been a pleasure to work with, Gabe. You and your mom. I'll continue to check in on you while you're here."

My mom and I expressed our thanks for his time. Dr. Weiss left the room. A few hours later a different, more equip nurse brought me breakfast. I decided I'd eat it. Since I'd been unable to eat much the past few days for the fear of vomiting it all back up again I needed something to keep me strong.

The next day or two went by fleetingly. Darla and Tony both came by to spend time with me. Darla brought me cookies that her mom had baked, and a book that her dad had read and thought that I'd enjoy reading to pass the time when I was alone. Tony brought a board game that he and I used to play when we were young. He thought it might be nice to feel nostalgic. I must admit that it was.

I had been moved to a nice private room with a window to the courtyard just outside. It was still winter so the trees were fairly barren, but it was still a beautiful view of my little piece of North Carolina.

The second night in my room Darla brought me a book her dad wanted me to read. It was a book about a young man who began living his life to the fullest when he was threatened with a life or death situation.

As I began fingering through the front matter of the book, I came upon the quote page. It read:

*"Someone should tell us, right at the start of our lives that we are dying. Then we might live life to the limit, every minute of every day. Do it, I say! Whatever you want to do, do it now! There are only so many tomorrows."*
*-Pope Paul IV*

Underneath the quote was a note written by Darla.

*Gabe,*
*My dad had asked me about giving this book to you around the time of the fair, but I thought it was too depressin, and way too similar to what you were going through. A week ago I flipped through the pages and saw the quote. It nearly broke my heart, but only because it's exactly what you have*

*shown me about life. Even though I've only had a couple of months to share with you as your girlfriend, you have forever changed my life. The kisses we shared were too few. (I know I'll day dream about those often ;) hehehe), and I'll never quite enjoy kicking rocks at another boy's ankles like I do yours.*

*The most important thing I want you to know is that I'll never regret loving you. The pain of losing you is far outweighed by the light your love has placed in my life.*

*Your Cocoa Butter,*
*Darla*

Jeez, Darla, way to make a guy cry. I loved that girl beyond my own understanding, but somehow I think she loved me even more. I planned to call her in the morning. To kiss those pretty lips at least one more time.

# Then

I was there with him.

He may not have known it, but I'd been around for quite some time before he even found out he had cancer. I knew that my mission this time around wasn't to help someone overcome a battle, but rather to live life to the fullest while waiting for the battle to cease.

Gabe had guided me just as much as I guided him.

In the middle of a January night not too many days after he'd been admitted to the hospital for consistent care, he drifted off to sleep and never woke up. He was still there though, his heart still beating, his lungs still breathing, but when someone would go to speak to him or shook him to see if he would respond, he wouldn't. I watched as nurses came in to check on him. I watched as they reassured his mom that he was still here and that if she spent time with him, he would know that she was there with him. He was definitely there, but I don't know how much he was aware of the life going on around him. It was as though his body was functioning, but his mind wouldn't connect with it.

It was a slow disconnection between his soul and body.

I sat there and stared at the boy I'd came to guide. I sat there in the corner and stared as his mom wept at his bedside. His beautiful girlfriend visited long hours, as did his spunky friend. His girlfriend had hopes that he was some type of 'Sleeping Beauty' and that if she kissed him he might wake up. Of course no matter how many times she tried he never shook the sleep. His best friend would sit by his side and would stick cigarettes in Gabe's mouth as well as his own. He wouldn't even light them, but he considered it a way of sharing nostalgia. It would only last until a nurse would come in and yank them away.

The people filtered in and out. They weren't just composed of his girlfriend, mom, and best friend; they were all of those around him who were affected by his battle.

Sometimes we assume that the battles we go through are all about us and our path of life. There's no other assumption that could be further from the truth. Often times the battles in our own lives are placed there simply to affect the others around us.

Yes we may be the ones who deal head on with the consequences and yes we may be the ones who feel the immediate pain, but the ones around us are often impacted just as tragically as we are. We often lack the ability to see the world from an external viewpoint.

One morning, just a few nights into February the monitors lit up and sounded the death toll. I watched as his soul left his body. His aura of light waved goodbye to me and drifted upwards.

His mom was in the room and shouted for the nurses as the lights on the monitors flashed. Medical staff rushed into the room to try and aid in keeping him within their world, but to no avail.

It's not to say they didn't give it all they had to help revive him, but somewhere in their own soul, they knew that his time had come. 'Long before anyone's life should end', many of them said.

If you ask me it ended just on time. At fifteen years old he had impacted more people than most adults have the opportunity to impact in their entire lifetime. People in his town and many towns over felt love and empathy towards a boy they hadn't even known of. His battle helped heal the hearts of many.

He and I had many conversations with one another. I knew firsthand the impact he had on the world. I also knew the impact that God had on his life towards the end. I feel fortunate enough myself to have been sent as a vessel for God because he even helped my spirit grow more.

His mom sat in the corner of his room hours after the nurses had tried to revive him. She even sat there hours after his body had been taking away. Though I knew she thought Gabe saw me because of his tumor, I also knew that this was going to be the biggest battle of her life.

I watched her sitting in a chair as she kicked her shoes off of her feet and brought them in towards her chest. She curled herself into a ball and stared at her son's empty bed. It broke my heart to watch her sit alone fighting back her tears.

"Sheila," I said, as I revealed myself to her.

She looked around and when her eyes landed on me they widened and glazed over.

"Sheila," I said again. "I'm Zippy."

"You're..." she said with tears trailing down her face.

I ran over to her and hugged her shoulders. "I'm your son's angel," I wiped a tear off of her cheek, "and now I'm here to be yours."

# About the Author

C.B. grew up a gypsy at her parents hands. With a dad in the Air Force she was able to experience life on the road, while soaking up culture. She enjoys any endeavors which aid in the expansion of the creative mind. Currently residing an hour outside of 'HotLanta', she lives with her husband, daughter, and bobtail cat, Sushi.

Keep up with C.B.:
CBBurdette.Blogspot.com
Or find her on GoodReads.com as C.B. Burdette

www.ingramcontent.com/pod-product-compliance
Lightning Source LLC
Chambersburg PA
CBHW020246180626
46810CB00006B/2389